Spittin' 'Em Out Like BABIES

THE WRITE MESSAGE

Library of Congress Control Number: 2008925742
ISBN-13: 978-0-9815668-1-8
ISBN-10: 0-9815668-1-2

Printed in the United States of America
10 9 8 7 6 5 4 3 2 1

Email: karlabkr@yahoo.com
www.facebook.com/karla.d.baker

Other books by Karla Denise Baker:

Anonymous

Sleepin' Wit' the Virus (a sequel to Anonymous)

To the young girl who confided in me
Know that your voice has been heard loud and clear.

For any young girl who has experienced this kind of pain. If
no one ever told you that they're sorry.

I'm Sorry
this happened to you.

(I must forewarn you this book is very explicit in detail.
Parental discretion is advised.)

"There is such a bed of black roses
A life of heartache and wretchedness
I am a sounding voice for those
who've pricked their tiny fingers
with spike thorns
bleeding to be believed."

Quote from: **Mrs. Bernice's sixth grade class**

"When a man makes you cum you should feel like you want
to soak his juices up like a sponge and fuck him like there's
no tomorrow. But if a hustler makes you cum know that he
won't only hustle you outta your cum. He will hustle you
outta your heart and soul believing that he gives a damn
about your muthafuckin' ass. Know this, he doesn't give a
damn 'bout you! It's about him getting his nutt. And once he
gets his that loser will make your hungry pussy starve."

Quote from: **Pink Khocolate**

Spittin'

'Em

Out

Like

BABIES

WM Publishing House, New York, NY

"Hello, sir, package for Mr. Jennings." The short white man with mousy-brown hair dressed in a chocolate brown uniform says, waiting for me to respond.

"Yes, that would be me." I say in an upbeat tone.

The man extends his pad out, "Sign here, please?"

I lean in and sign on the dotted line and then reach out to take the package. I proceed to shut the door behind me.

Normally I would be pushing the DOWN button to the elevator and heading home, but not today. Today, I chose to wait for a particular package to arrive from literary agent, Julie Flight. I mean Julie talked it up so much that it left me curious as to what the manuscript is about.

As I am about to open the package the darn phone rings.

Ring, Ring…

I snatch it up with my right hand. "Hello, Jennings."

"Hi, sweetie, you still at the office, huh, what time will you be coming home?"

"Soon, baby, soon."

EMBELLISH B.

I member back in the second grade this Puerto Rican kid named Elvis Rodriguez told this little black gurl to suck his *wee-wee* all because she wouldn't share a piece of Bazooka bubble gum wit' him during recess. Well, the little black gurl ran and told our teacher and Elvis was sent to the principal's office. The principal and Elvis later returned back to our classroom. The principal made Elvis apologize to the little girl in front of the whole class. Talk about humiliated.

Well, short dark-haired tan-skinned Elvis had his head bowed like he was remorseful. The little gurl was sitting in the front row of the class staring at him. Elvis raised his head and stared at the brown-eyed gurl and he began to stutter out his words in broken English, "sor-ry for tella you to sucka my *wee-wee*."

He turned in the principal's direction wit' a puppy dog look in his eyes and a sulk upon his face, but when he turned facing the class he had a devious expression of revenge. All of a sudden, Elvis yanked down his navy-blue high-water corduroy pants and pulled out his Vienna sausage looking pinkish-colored *thang* and said, "*Mami*, sucka my dick!"

Elvis was pulling hard on the shriveled up little fellah. Well, the teacher and principal's face turned beet red. The little black gurl just stared at the little fellah in shock. The rest of the class burst out into laughter. Well, this massive hand snatched Elvis's ear and twist it as it turned fire engine red and escorted him out of the classroom.

I don't have to tell y'all what happened to Elvis Rodriguez, now do I? But I often wondered whatever happened to that little black gurl. I mean did she ever grow up sucking dick? My inquiring mind was dying to know.

I member as a little black gurl livin' in the Broke-Down Housing Projects in New York these life insurance peoples (four white men's) had come in front of my building try'na gets me to buy insurance policies. They was all dressed like church boys.

I said, "Yo', can't you see I'ma kid."

The blonde-haired men's said, "Well, do you have parents?"

What kind of stupid ass question was that, I thought to myself.

I swayed my head no.

"Well, do you have siblings?" The red-faced freckled man axed, while the other two dark-haired men's waited fo me to respond.

"Siblings? What's a sibling," I thought to myself. *Why he using big words?*

"Talk English," I snapped wit' my little hands on my pint-sized hips. And he talked realllllllll slow like I jus' got off the yellow bus or something.

The red-faced man repeated hisself. "Do you have brothers or sisters?"

I swayed my head no.

He never let up. I figured this white dude musta jus' got this job 'cause he seemed hungry. Why they in the 'hood anyways? I wondered. *Wha' we need wit' life insurance*, I thought.

Man, I laughed in all four of their faces. They didn't care. They jus' kept on preachin' like those peoples who come to yo house uninvited and as soon as you open the door you see the whole goddamn family standing in front of you smiling 'n shit and it be like 8:00 in the morning. You figured they would see that you be dead tired, but they don't give a fuck. They jus' wanna chitchat 'bout G-Man and whatnot.

I 'member one short, black woman axed me if I knew God. I shrugged my shoulders 'cause it wasn't like He lived down the hall from me.

"What you mean?" I axed her, while wiping my red eyes.

The same woman said, "Do you have a relationship with God?"

I frowned 'cause that sounded *nasty*. "No, bitch, God gotta dickey and I don't like dickeys!" I snapped.

Her big eyes liked to pop outta her head. I guess she knew what "*dickey*" meant. She jus' ought to being around here. I didn't care. I slammed the door in all their faces. Then I questioned, why would I be *stroking* God? "She stupid," I said to myself and had gone back to bed, but I couldn't sleep. That woman had me up all fuckin' night, thankin'.

You see I figured when the time came fo me to go to Blues City (that's what I called Heaven) God would already know 'bout my life history. Heck, He wrote the book. I figured we, God and me would chitchat over a shot of gin and pizza. Yeah. Talk 'bout all the mistakes I'd made on earth as a dysfunctional confused black gurl. And I would more than likely ax Him, "Yo' G-Man, if you knew that this shit was gonna happen to me, why didn't You stop it? Why lemme suffer?" And G-Man would more than likely shrug his broad shoulders looking all dumbfounded as if to say, "I dunno, dummy. Wha' you think I'm God?"

And I would sarcastically say, "Well, who da fuck is You then if You ain't God?"

9

And G-Man would stick up his middle finger as if to say, "Fuck you, bitch."

Just by His behavior I wondered if G-Man smoked crack 'cause He was actin' weird 'n shit.

Yep. That's how I pictured my talk wit' G-Man. Like I said, I wassa kid. But kid or not, I hated boys and Lawd knows I hated me some *dickey*!

***

KNOCK-BOOTS, NY

I had a boyfriend named Tyler Watson. Dang. He was deep dark complected. Tyler was different 'cause he was born wit' one brown eye and one hazel eye. And he was *fine*. His eyes were dreamy eyes. Special eyes. He had a wide nose and perfect shaped lips. He stood about 5'6" wit' dreams of becoming a doctor. We both had dreams. I wanted to be a makeup artist and travel around the world wit' artists like: Madonna. Prince. Sheila E. The Pointer Sisters. Yeah, it was kinda bittersweet.

Tyler and I had a lot in common 'cause he didn't have a father either. His momma worked hard to provide him wit' clothes, shoes, all the thangs a boy would need. He was her only chile. Nah. He wasn't spoiled or nuthin'. Tyler was easygoing. I felt bad that his momma couldn't give him another daddy. I didn't know why. It coulda been 'cause he was a 13½-year-old boy. Yeah, I thought 'bout who he was gonna have as a role model. You know a father figure. There weren't many sober men's acting out the role of "Daddy" 'round the way.

Unfortunately, Tyler's Dad was killed back in 1972. Yeah, some thugs tried to rob him while he was waiting for a bus. He was working his second shift job at Home Depot. You know try'na provide for the fam. He was working in Union, New Jersey. Well, these thugs stuck him up and Tyler's dad only had like four dollars on him. He had jus' paid the rent so he was dead broke. Jokers wasn't try'na hear it. They wanted him to shit some loot out of his ass, if he had to. He jus' had betta' come up wit' some more loot and quick. Poor man ain't have no more loot so it was like kiss yo last breath good-bye muthafucka. POP, POP, POP, POP! They slung four bullets in him and then dragged his stout body in the back of an abandoned building. He bled to death. They didn't find his decomposed body until two weeks after his murder.

Tyler shared that story wit' me so many times I knew the shit *verbatim* (I learned that word "verbatim" from Mrs. Bernice class.) Tyler usedta keep a newspaper clipping of the article in his backpack. I didn't know why. The paper was all yellow and crumpled, but he didn't care. He'd fold it neatly and tuck it back in his backpack. He said his momma had given it to him. Now, why would she do some dumb shit like that? Your guess was as good as mine. It seemed like it did him mo' harm, than good. I could hear it in his voice. Saw it in his eyes. The pain was still real to him.

Well, as fo me, my dreary tale was that Daddy-O jetted. Fuck *'im*! *He's probably a bum anyways.*

***

When Bedell was sixteen she had Pretty-Boy. I came

strolling along four years later. Yep. Another bastard was born. For some reason our Daddy never wanted to tie the knot wit' her. You know make her a wife 'n shit. Bedell wassa good catch. He musta been blind as a bat. But he couldn't have been too blind 'cause he ain't have no problem knocking her ass up and leaving her to fend fo herself and us. That usedta piss me off every time she tried to get in contact wit' his stingy ass. It could've been an emergency and he wouldn't even pick up the damn phone to find out what was going on. I usedta get tired of seeing Bedell eyes well up. Ooh... that shit usedta irk my last nerve! It made me wanna pop a cap in his ass if I ever saw him. That punk-ass nigga wasn't *shit* in my book. Shit! I didn't care if he helped out here and there. The only reason that happened was because Bedell had to practically beggggggg him to take care of his bastards. I woulda tooken his sorry ass to the "white man" and called it a fuckin' day, but Bedell didn't get down like that. She was too damn nice fo her own fuckin' good. She was breaking her back, working two jobs 'cause she let pride get in her way. Fuck pride! We had to eat! We needed shit and wit' her two jobs it still wasn't putting a dent in thangs that had to get done. We were scraping the bottom of the jelly jar jus' to survive. Eaten mayonnaise sandwiches and drinking sugared water 'cause we ain't have no damn Kool-Aid. C'mon! So yeah, Tyler and I had that in common: big dreams and no damn fuckin' daddies. Nobody wanted to be livin' in the 'hood, forever. I sho' as hell didn't. It was more to life than this shit.

Tyler's mom, Mrs. Watson took it hard fo long time mourning over the loss of her dead husband. She let herself go. She started lookin' rundown. Beat down...sounds betta'. Wasn't nobody try'na kick it to her lookin' like shit. She gained all this extra weight.

She just looked busted and disgusted. But after 'bout three months something changed in Mrs. Watson. She started working out. Walking in the mornin' before she headed off to her job at Walmart. She was lookin' spiffy like she had met someone. Uh-huh. She was even wearing makeup and had gone and bought herself some wigs. Uh-huh. I sniffed *dick* all over this new and improved Mrs. Watson.

But I was wayyyyyyyyyy off base—ya heard.

I had heard around the way that Mrs. Watson was kickin' it a'ight. She was being wined and dined by this dyke named Coochie Browne. It blew my mind when I heard that Mrs. Watson was now Coochie's *bitch*. Everybody knew Coochie—straight up butch. Yeah, she usedta be on the block of Curbstone makin' her hustle. Word of mouth traveled that Coochie had mad paper. She jus' acted like she didn't so she could collect that "crazy men's" check by the first of the month. I didn't know if Tyler got word or not. And I sho' as hell wasn't gonna tell him. How da fuck was I 'sposed to tell my first real love that his momma jumped the motherfuckin' fence? Answer that?! I ain't know how to break the news to him. That was some heavy shit to unload on a brotha. Nah. I couldn't do it. Not to him. I loveded that boy too much to mess my shit up fo Mrs. Watson—that fat bitch was on her own. You feel me?

But then it was like WHOA! The freakin' earth shook or something. Tyler's mom was hooked on Coochie. I ain't say COCK. I said COOCHIE.

Coochie was a man to naked eye even though deep down she was a woman or vice-verse. She was confused, if you axed me. Coochie had a husky voice and usedta loveded to hold her crotch like she had a big dick. She usedta kill me wit' that shit.

While Mrs. Watson was gettin' her groove on wit' Coochie, Tyler still had no clue of what da fuck was goin' on. 'Ey, I wasn't gonna be the one to break his heart. Why? Yooo', 'cause I ain't never seent a boy cry before, but Tyler wasn't afraid to cry in front of me. I was the one all tight faced, afraid to let my emotions flow. I never shed a tear in front of him. Tyler was going through a lot and I guess Mrs. Watson was preoccupied. I became his shoulder to lean on. I was his ear to listen to his problems. I was his arm to console him in his time of need. I was his gurl. I had to be his first real love. Why? 'Cause he showed me his vulnerable side, that's the fuck why. He showed me and it touched me way deep in my heart. I loveded that boy fo real.

Tyler and I ain't never gets busy. You know, doin' da nasty. Nah. He ain't never had a taste of my skins. He never touched me inappropriately. He was a true gentleman. True. The closest we'd come to smooching was me giving him a peck on the cheek fo walking me home from school. And he even carried my books. He was so polite. I was the luckiest gurl on the block of Layton and Brower. But then lucky turned into unlucky in love.

Tyler and I attended P.S. 3 and we had a half a day that particular Thursday. Well, Tyler walked me home and then headed home on DuMont and 33rd. He liveded in a nice house wit' a lotta trees 'n shit. He opened the door to his house, walked inside and heard some noises, so he yelled out fo his momma. But she didn't answer. He kept hearing sounds comin' from his mother's bedroom so he pushed the ajar door slightly only to witness his momma in the act of gettin' her coochie eaten out by Coochie. It startled 'em all. Well, not Coochie. She ain't give a flying fuck.

Well, Tyler dashed out of the bedroom and frantically called me. He was rambling at first. And then he got to the point of what had happened. He told me everythang. He was in shock. He kept repeating it over and over. "Embellish, eaten COOCHIE coochie MOMMA!"

I was like, "WHOA, brotha! That's too much information fo me."

It was too much fo Tyler to stomach so he ran out of the house like his body was caught on fire. He dashed across Curbstone so fast wit'out paying attention and had gotten hit by an eighteen-wheeler. The news was earth shattering as one of our friends ran to my house to tell me.

I dashed out of the house wit' no coat on. I ran so fast that the wintry breeze had to catch up wit' me. My arms were swinging back and forth, palms were balled, legs were like a thoroughbred on the racetracks trampling through the hills of snow and my feet were slipping and sliding on the covered white pavement wit' sweat streaming down my face and under my armpits. I was try'na to get there in time.

Once I got to Curbstone, it was OVER.

Tyler—his face embedded in the bloody red slush. His left arm sprawled upward like a wing of an angel, his right arm bent and twisted like a corkscrew; both of his legs were mangled like metal, and blood. Oh man, Tyler was smothered in blood wit' splattered brains all the way down to his torso. It was a gruesome scene. Tyler was dead. And I nearly losted my damn mind eyeballing it all.

A crowd swung around the corner of Curbstone to view the grisly scene. My body was trembling as I heard folks whispering. I felt emotions building in me. I was in shock. Tyler...Tyler. It was so unexpected, but so real to my eyes. Oh, I wanted to cry but I couldn't. I wondered why. Why wouldn't I cry fo my first real love? I knew in my heart that Tyler was on his way to my house. Unfortunately, he never made it due to the driver of that eighteen-wheeler being a fuckin' lush. It was some messed up shit 'cause while Tyler's guts were splattered all over the streets, Mrs. Watson was home gettin' her pussy licked. It hurt me deeply, so deep that I losted my way. I started cutting school, smokin' weed, and drinking Smooth Dawg. Now that shit will make yo' titties feel like they on fire. I was at the end of my rope. I marked that day on my calendar. Tyler Watson died on November 11th 1984. My first real love was dead. Special eyes. Tyler Watson was deadddddddddddd!

Once Mrs. Watson got word, she wasn't the same since. She ended up in one of those loony bins and hadn't been seent since. I was deep into Tyler 'cause he was different. He knew what he wanted and how he was gonna get it. He treated me special. And after his death, I was giving up on life. I was wounded. I had never experienced that form of love before even though it was short-liveded. Tyler would always have a special part of my heart. Since his death, I hadn't been the same. I guessed you could say I was giving up too. If only Tyler could come back it coulda been a strong possibility that I coulda been that gurl again. But those days were gone. Tyler Watson was gone and so was I.

Guilt was creepin' on me so heavy. It was tiptoeing back so quietly into my life. I had a confession to make to Tyler. It hurt to even think about it. It hurt so, so badly.

I stared out of my bedroom window into the violet sky and I said in the softest tone I could muster up. "Tyler, I knew that cat...drunk driver. We went waaaayyyyy back. Yeah, *back* in that same eighteen-wheeler. Yo Tyler, listen it's a long story—a dark memory of my past." And I swore I heard Tyler's voice say, "Embellish, tell me what happened? I'm listening." God, I swore on my momma that Tyler spoke to me. It spooked me out!

I lowered my head feeling so ashamed, but I knew it was time to let my titties hang. Trust me, I ain't wanna, but something deep inside kept gnawing at me. I think it was my conscience eatin' at my pain. What else could it be? I axed myself. What else?

***

When I was eleven I was full of life. I loveded to horseplay wit' Pretty-Boy. Eleven was a good age—a happy age. I never really talked about my blood brother anymore. I never talked about him 'cause he wasn't worth talkin' about. He wasn't worth shit! He wasn't shit in my book. Shit, shit, shit! *This was gonna be the last time I talks him up,* I thought to myself. THE LAST!!!!

I loveded Pretty-Boy to death. I would've given up a kidney fo him. I would've given blood, if he was deathly ill. I would've even eaten his pigs feet that he hated jus' so he could get dessert. That's how much I loveded him. He was like a young daddy since our daddy was gone. I had never had the pleasure of meeting the muthafucka. Nah.

When Bedell had Pretty-Boy she told me she struggled wit' him being single and all. From all the stories Bedell had it's a wonder why she never gave him up fo adoption. Bedell said that she couldn't give her chile up fo adoption jus' 'cause our daddy jetted didn't mean she had to abandon him too. Pretty-Boy and I were inseparable. He was my protector. My big brother-father.

But something changed between us that February. I couldn't understand what. Pretty-Boy started beating me given me black and blue eyes. Purple bruises on my neck. He started bullying me hard. I even caught him spying on me, while I was using the bathroom doing number 2. He was actin' weird. All I knew was that he became a different brother-father and I tried to ignore him. I thought maybe some gurl had him pussy whipped. I didn't know what had changed.

But one day I looked in the full-length cracked mirror in my bedroom and I saw that *I* had changed. The once skinny rail was filling out that body of mine. Bedell hadn't made collard greens, grits and home fries, cornbread or banana pudding in weeks, so how come I was gettin' thick? I shrugged my shoulders. I was justa kid. How the hell was I 'sposed to know?

Anyways, we continued to horseplay, but Pretty-Boy always wanted to do it in my bedroom. We usedta have lots of fun, but then things turned ugly. Pretty-Boy's thin fingers slithered in my flowery panties and "Oh, brother-father" took on a whole new meaning in my life.

***

"Ow…Pretty-Boy, you hurtin' me! Stop! Sssstop. I'ma tell Momma. I don't wanna play no mo'." My eyes were the size of gumballs, begging fo him to stop. But he wouldn't listen.

"Shhh. You betta' not tell nobody or else." He said in his controlling voice. He'd emphasized "or else" quite often. And then he would ball his fists real big and mush me in my face. He put fear in my heart. And I never told a soul, not even Bedell. He threatened to kill me. He wouldn't stop.

"Open your legs!" He'd snap, as his two fingers

opened the lips to my little pussy and he'd moan as his finger rubbed my clitoris back and forth like a pencil eraser. He damn near rubbed my skin raw. Then he got some ice cubes and inserted them inside of me called hisself being romantic. I considered him sick. He stuck it inside of me, as far as it would go with his jagged nails.

"OOOOWWW Pretty-Boy!" I screamed like lava was burning my flesh. It hurt. It huuuurrrrrrrt so bad. I bled heavy. I didn't know if my period had started at eleven or not. I didn't know where the blood was coming from. Pretty-Boy never stopped to take me to the doctor or to the hospital. He never stopped to tell Bedell. He never stopped to shake that demon outta him. Make up a lie or something. Nah. He just kept on doin' me.

By the next day the madness continued.

"C'mere." He said, while standing inside the door of my bedroom. I rose to my feet still half asleep. Bedell had gone to the store.

"Lift up your shirt. Take off that training bra. Lemme see them titties. Damn Embellish, they gettin' big and plump. Oooooooooh. Slop, slop, slop," his lips and tongue made that kind of sound as he licked 'em like a thirsty dog. He pulled my nipples wit' his sharp teeth and broke the skin.

"OOOOOWWWWWWWW Pretty-Boy that hurt!" I shrieked.

"Shut up! It don't hurt...it feels good to you. Lay your pretty ass down and open up." I heard him unzip his pants and then I saw his hard dick staring at me. I turned my head, looked down to stare at the floor. I cut my eyes to the sides' try'na block out the image of that long pipe between his legs and those two black eyeballs staring back at me.

"Sit up." He'd demanded, while holding his dick in

his right hand.

So I sat up.

"Open your mouth."

So I opened my mouth as wide as I could and said, "Ahhhhhhhhhhhhhhhhhhhhhh."

"Taste it, lick it, and suck it."

So I stuck out my lizard-sized tongue and licked the sides like an ice cream cone.

"No, listen when I tell you something! Now TASTE it! All of it." The look on his face was serious. Those dark eyes burnt through my thin skin. I swallowed down the rocks in my throat. Pretty-Boy was damn near a grown ass man.

"C'MERE! Here!" He pointed to the tip of his dick. "Put it in your mouth."

My chocolate-colored eyes spread wide as the pink barrettes that dangled from my ponytails slapped me in the face as I vigorously shook my head no. With quick reflexes his backhand collided with my face, SMACK! I was woozy like he had knocked the wind outta me.

"Put it in your mouth or else!"

I was still woozy as I trembled in my skin.

He moved closer.

"Get on your knees."

So I got on my knees.

"Open your mouth and suck." He leaned his head back waiting for the moisture from my mouth to touch his thick skin.

"SUC-CK, BIT-CH, SUC-CCCK!" He'd snapped.

I flinched and then closed my eyes as he shoved his dick in my mouth. I nearly gagged to death.

"Look, I ain't got all day." His dark eyes pierced at the gutted hole in the wall. "Open your mouth wide. Wet them pretty lips."

I burst into tears, loud and then soft.

"Shut da hell up! SHUT IT UP-P! I don't wanna

hear no whining. Stop that cryin'. You'sa big gurl and big gurls do thangs like this to they brothers. It's good. Feels good!"

I looked up at him and the tears rolled down my weary face. I HATED HIM. He was the only one who could make me cry.

"You love me don' you?"

I nodded my head up and down wit' wet and dry tears streaked on my small face.

"Open your mouth, again, but this time wider." He balled his fists real big.

My eyes stared at those balled fists. And I did. I opened my mouth wide outta fear.

"Stick out your tongue. Lemme see some spit. Do your lips like dis. LOOK!" He pouted his chapped lips. "Act sexy. Act like you sexy. You know how the gurls look on them Playboy magazines."

I shrugged my shoulders 'cause I didn't know how. I didn't know what Playboy was.

"Do it jus' like them."

I had to think quickly on my feet. So I tried to mimic them but I wasn't sure if I had it down pat. I pouted and poked out my dry lips, gave him sexy looks, stuck out my little ass, jiggled my tittics, stuck out my tongue, and glossed my lips wit' spit. And again, I did it all outta fear as I shivered the whole time.

"Oooooooh," he grinned and jumped up and down like he had won on the Price-Is-Right. "Whew! I knew you had it in you, E! Put your tongue here." He pointed to the head of his dick. "LICK!" He moaned and then tilted his head back, wet his lips, and bit down hard on his bottom lip like he was gonna fuck the shit outta me. His hand palmed the top of my head like a Spalding basketball and he squeezed it like a pimple as my eyes flooded wit' emotion wondering why he was doing this to me—his blood sister.

"Suck it hard. Deep-throat it." He said, and kept his eyes closed, waiting.

I looked up at him and my eyes were pleading to stop the madness. They were big watery eyes. And again, I shrugged my shoulders 'cause I didn't know what *deep-throat* was. I almost vomited my guts out as he forced me to swallow his dick whole. My eyeballs felt like they were going to pop outta my head. I couldn't fit him in my mouth. He was waaaayyyy too big.

"DO IT AGAIN, BIT-CH!" His backhand spoke, WHACK, right on top of my head. Tears leaked out of my eyes. I was broken. I couldn't. I was tired, so, so very tired. My jaws were locking up on me. But Pretty-Boy didn't care. He had me on my knees fo hours until they literally turned black.

I was experiencing years of *nasty* from Pretty-Boy. He coulda had any gurl he wanted wit' that gorgeous cashmere brown skin, doe-eyes, and that butter teeth smile. He had that long Indian-like hair that he kept in a ponytail. Most gurls considered him fine, but not me. Pretty-Boy was fixated wit' me. Maybe 'cause he could control me, put fear in me. He taught me that *beauty* lies between my legs. He taught me to groom my beauty. To caress *it*. To feed *it* when it was hungry. To taste *it* wit' my finger. To pleasure *it* wit' porn. He taught me how to ride him like a cowgirl. He taught me how to make that poppin' sound wit' my mouth while I was sucking his dick. He taught me how to lick his balls. He taught me how to make *him* feel good. He called me names: slut, hoe, skank, bitch, dick-pleaser and said that I was a damned good one.

At that point I knew that my life was over. I was hooked on *dick* like it was meth, crack, coke, and heroin. I loveded dick. I loveded it mo' than life. I was so caught up that I didn't know how to stop. I wanted to stop, I think. But how? I couldn't keep my legs clamped or my mouth shut. I had to have dick or I would go damn crazy. I hated crazy. I had heard what crazy could do to yah. It was scary to me. I had to fuck. So I did. And I didn't care where I got it.

Things got so bad that I started sucking bums dick jus' to feed the cravings. The homeless became my regulars. And the winos I usedta slop 'em up and spit that nasty aftertaste outta my mouth. Those muthafuckas smelt like road kill. Just imagine that taste on your tongue, *Eew!*

I was so young and so vulnerable. I felt like I had a drug running through my veins that made me do it. It wasn't me, not totally. Pretty-Boy. He took all of my innocence away from me. He stole my childhood and darkened and tarnished it fo bad. Killing me hard, not softly. HARD.

I did everythang hard: I fucked hard. I lost hard. I talked hard. I liveded hard. Everything was hard. I was too hard to love.

After a few years of being tortured I noticed that March that my stomach was swelling up like a small cantaloupe. Then the size of a honeydew. It was too much to face so I ran away before Bedell got wind. Bedell was frantic. And truthfully, I didn't care. Bedell never filed a missing person report on me, though. And I always questioned, why? I started doubting if she loveded me enough. I thought she forgot about me. Stopped loving me.

Anyways, I hooked up wit' my gurl, Manhattan Mansfield. She usedta live in Broke-Down Housing Projects, too. That's where we met, but as she got older her momma moved to Jersey City, New Jersey. I crashed wit' her until I had...*it*. I thought of Bedell. I missed her, but I hated her. Yeah. I had mixed emotions. Well, since I ran away one of Manhattan's aunts pretended to be my guardian. November 11th *it* was born. *I* didn't name *it*. *I* didn't want to see *it*. *I* wanted to forget *it*. The only reason I chose to spare *its* life was 'cause Bedell spared mine. Bedell did the best she could fo me and wit' nuthin' I tried to do the best I could fo *it*.

Afterwards, I had to live wit' the memory of *it* being a product of *his* poison, and within my skin I grieved fo my loss. I let *it* rest in peace. And I moved on wit' my life.

After recuperating, I returned back to Knock-Boots as if nuthin' ever happened. Yep. Muthafucka was the word.

Tyler. Tyler was the only *good* that I had in my life. Everythang had stopped by the time I met Tyler. Pretty-Boy's poison was outta me. Pretty-Boy was gone. Yeah, Pretty-Boy got tied up in some *investments*. I was starting over. My pain was outta sight, outtaf mind. There was no need fo me to tell Tyler 'bout my past. Tyler was breath of fresh air. He got me away from the dark side of myself. I felt so blessed to have him. But I was livin' a double life. I was bad blood. I felt nasty most of the time, 'cept in his presence. Tyler took me away from the bullshit of the streets. He made me dream. And after he died I dreamt that I was betta' than nasty—that I was a good nasty wit' perfume pussy.

I'ma share something wit y'all.

The drunk driver that killed Tyler was one of my clients. #66. I gave all of my clients' numbers 'cause I kept forgetting their fuckin' names. I was always good wit' numbers so it seemed easier fo me to remember. Yeah, I had many numbers. Jus' *spittin' 'em out like babies*.

But my world crumbled when I saw #66s face and Tyler smashed in the ground. I completely lost it inside. My heart plummeted to my feet. It seemed like anythang that I had ever loveded turned rotten, including me. I became a nymphomaniac. Jus'a fuckin' machine. Mornin', noon, and night...jus' fuckin' to keep my mind off of my troubles and some loot in my Gucci bag.

I was broken and Bedell ain't know shittttt! There was no hope fo me. Nah. I was terminal like AIDS.

Between the death of Tyler and the molestation or what some called *incest* or *rape* from Pretty-Boy, and the death of that little black girl (me) I trusted no one. Not even myself. I looked at men's fo what they were worth: MONEY/DICK/DICK/MONEY. I stopped believing in love a long time ago. I stopped believing in dreams. I stopped believing in me. I pulled the plug and shut down to the point of no return.

My relationship wit' Bedell had changed. I grew bitterly angry wit' Momma and she didn't even know it. How come she didn't know, I wondered? How come? Bedell gave birth to his muthafucking ass. How come she couldn't tell that something was wrong?! HOW COME SHE DIDN'T KNOW THAT HER DEMENTED SON WAS FUCKIN' HER DAUGHTER?! HIS SISTER! I wanted to cry so badly, but the tears would not form. Shittttt.

I had to grow up faster than my years 'cause of him. I got thicker. Titties got bigger taking up most of my chest area. Ass grew higher and apple-shaped. I was an eye-catcher. No. I wassa fuckin' goddess. My hips looked like two bowling balls wit' a big ass *gap* in between my legs, wearing a size two frame. The hood-rats hated me 'cause their *dicks* were fiend fo me. I was the special of the year. My hair, I cut low and the white men's were hungry fo my pink khocolate. Shit I reminded 'em of being on a Caribbean island somewhere. They loveded that shit. I wore makeup to accentuate my pretty ass and glossed those moneymaking lips jus' 'nough to gloss some dicks down as I sucked 'em hard and dry.

Men...they had a liken fo me 'cause I wasn't a teaser. I was a DICK PLEASER. But it came wit' some real shit. Yeah. Men's had a strong liken fo my body, first. My mind, they didn't even know my mind. They jus' wanted to fuck me outta my mind. Yeah, they jus' wanted to cum and go running home to their wives and girlfriends like they were being faithful 'nd shit. I had to eat that shit every day. Thicken my skin. Yeah. I wasn't no dumb bitch. I was smart. And I was gettin' paid like that fo a ghetto-chick. 'Ey, my name wasn't Embellish fo nuthin'. Ya heard.

But I was dumb in one instance 'cause I was using my real name. *Idiot!* That was the stupidest thang I had ever done. Goes to show I had a lot to learn about the game. So I pondered over what I would call myself. Hmmm. I stroked my chin. Since I was dark as creamy sweet chocolate and my clit was pretty pink like cotton candy I decided to call myself, Pink Khocolate, founder of Pussi Control, Inc. My motto: *"Caressing dicks that were hungry fo some pink clit."*

Y'all gotta understand Embellish B's bed was made fo her—me, so I knew I had to lie back in the muthafucker. I made my bread 'n butter on my back. Let my body works fo me. Let my legs open sesame to any and every uncaring, self-centered muthafucker who didn't whisper sweet nuthins in my ears. Shit. They yelled, demanded, manipulated, and talked down to me, but yet in all I kept opening my legs 'cause it felt/feels bad/good to me. Hmm. It was all I had, all I knew.

BAD/BAD/BAD.
FUCK/FUCK/FUCK.
MONEY/MONEY/MONEY.

It was a hellacious way to live. See, I ain't ashamed to say that I pretended many a nights that I was being pleasured wit' make-believe love. You know, the kind of love that caressed good pussy—makin' it feel extra good. That shit felt real to me, you know? It was so vivid where I thought I could see myself opening up to a good dick that was attached to a good lovin' man. But no! All I got was those paper-clip rejects. And I'd fantasize about a good dick massaging my tension away. Yeah. One that would lick my pussy like I was a sweet chocolate kiss. Yeah sweet 'nough to *eat* me up wit' compassion. I craved a good dick that would share cumming, not cum wit'out me cumming. Yeah, a unselfish dick. I wanted that good dick to make me cum to the point where I thought I was an epileptic. You know, shaking, eyes rolling, and foaming at the mouth. You saw that chick in that movie, um, *Waist Deep* she had that shit down pat. That's how the fuck I wanted to feel. Jus' like that.

"Fuck me muthafucker!" I'd scream at the top of my lungs 'cause it felt so fuckin' good! Oooh! I could only wish that muthafucker would carry me over the threshold and take my ass far away from the slum and set my ass up nice 'n pretty in a house and feed my ass cheese omelets, fresh fruit, and toast like in *Love Jones* 'n shit. Darius got his shit off wit' that move.

I wanted to get away from all the many assortments of dick. I jus' wanted one flavor—Made-fo-Me. Yeah, some of those dicks didn't taste as good as they'd looked trust me. Again, I was dreaming hard, but I had nuthin' left but a dream 'cause from where I stood the slum was as good as it was gonna get fo a gurl likes me.

Okay…I basically handed in my "faith card" and dealt the hand that I was given. I made it work fo me and I was survivin' through all the bullshit on the outside, but inside I was shriveling up like a wrinkled old white lady.

***

Ring…Ring…Ring.

I flipped open the Pink BlackBerry knowing it was time to get down to business.

"Hel-loooo. What's your pleasurrree?" I spoke seductively as I was lying back in my office, (which was my bedroom closet) wit' my pretty feet resting on the dingy wall and my Dell laptop near my side.

"I'm craving something sweet. What's your rate?" A baritone voice spoke.

"Are you a referral?"

"Yes."

"Who?"

"Ah, 69."

"Ooh, that brings back memories." I smirked. "What you lookin' fo?"

"Um…I don't quite know. This is my first time."

I smirked.

This is going to be some easy cash, I thought to myself.

"Well, I can start you off slow and work my way up. How does that sound?" I pressed my ear to the phone. I could hear him breathing hard. "Where are you?" I axed. "What's your occupation?"

"Um…Um…I'm home, but you *can't* come *heere.*" He stuttered. "I'm a doctor."

"I wouldn't think of it. A doctor, you say. Listen, I can reserve a room at the Wilton Hotel in Queens. Are you familiar wit'?"

"Ah yes, quite."

"I need your credit card number fo collateral."

"Ahhhh."

He seemed hesitant. I needed to calm his nerves so I said, "This is business. My clients always cover fo the rooms. Trust me it will be worth your while. I spoke in an Eartha Kitt voice, "You sound like you are starvvvvving darling. Are you hungry? Mmmmmmmmmmmmmmmmm, 'cause I'm famished."

"Ahhhh, yes," he scratched his throat. "Yes, I'm quite hungry."

"Credit card number and type and expiration date, which do you have: Visa, MasterCard, American Express, Discover, puuulllllease?" I kept reeling him in.

"Um, it's ah, American Express. The card number is...and the expiration date is 11/11."

11/11. Images of Pretty-Boy appeared before my eyes. I quickly flinched back into character.

"O-Oh, could you give me the three digit security numbers on the back of your card?"

"Oh...526."

I scratched my throat. Then I proceeded to say, "Okay, I'll reserve the room under Pink Khocolate." I was already on the Internet making the reservation.

"Pink Khocolate," he repeated.

"Shall we say, in an hour? I wanna look eatable for you." I smiled slyly.

"An hour, okkkkkayyyyyyyy," he said nervously.

"Don't worry baby, I'm gonna take good care of you." Click.

As a "Khocolate Companion" I aimed to please. I crawled from out of the moth-scented closet in my small bedroom and planned out how I wanted that evening to be. I was very anal about detail. Very. If Bedell knew what I was doing she would have surely kicked me out. But she was at her second job so I was in the clear.

Look, I was try'na bank my loot until I had enough to get out of that dump. I didn't want to have to come crawling back home to Momma 'cause I ain't have enough loot stashed up. Once I left that roach motel it was a wrap.

I walked over and unzipped the plastic storage closet next to the second-hand, scratched up three-legged dresser and pulled out my Tory Burch dress and Versace sandals. I had no choice but to take a shower in that grungy bathroom and as soon as I stuck my leg in a little baby roach was crawling down the cracked tile. I grabbed a dry towel and whacked it real good. Then its momma came to join in the duel and I knocked her off and her unborn babies. Then a whole heap of roaches started marching down the line like they were in the military ready to do battle, so I wet the towel and *WHACK, WHACK, WHACK* until all their asses washed down the drain. I had to get myself together 'cause I was buggin' out.

"Shake it off, gurl," I said to myself.

Finally, I took my shower.

It was going on 9:00 p.m. by the time I got dressed, painted up my sexy, and looked myself over in my full-length cracked mirror.

I grabbed my Versace clutch bag, sprayed on some Coco Mademoiselle Chanel Paris on my neck and dabbed a little behind my ears. I almost forgot to unravel my Betsey Johnson scarf from my low 'do.

I grabbed my Coach traveling bag that was always prepared ahead of time and strutted out of the bedroom, out the door, stepped onto the elevator, and out the lobby door and walked towards the bus stop to catch the #24 bus to Murray Street to Mr. Rays Garage to hop in my Jaguar.

Mr. Rays was a middle-age man, medium build, short in height wit' a receding hairline and a sly grin that seemed painted on his scruffy looking face. He had a thang fo young gurls so I had to work my magic by flashing him one tit and bending over showing him the crack of my ass. That's all she wrote and Mr. Rays gave me the space in his garage fo free.

As long as I kept flashing his perverted ass I could keep the space so you know what I did, huh. 'Ey, a gurl had do what a gurl had to do.

I raised the door to garage #7 and there she was all pearly white staring back at me. Yep. My baby I named... Pleasure-Me-Down.

Pleasure-Me-Down purred up as I opened the trunk to put the traveling bag in, shut the trunk, and hopped in sinking into the soft butter-cream leather. Pleasure rode so smoothly, as usual. I pumped up the volume on the radio and started bopping my head to hip-hop beats.

I arrived at Wilton Hotel at approximately 9:52 p.m. I popped the trunk, grabbed my clutch bag, opened the car door, and stepped one leg out that was of sheer irradiance, then the other, and I stood, wiggled to shake the wrinkles out of my dress.

I walked to the back of the car and grabbed my traveling bag and strutted wit' a sway that was saying, "You ain't got shit on me," wit' such vainness.

I entered the luxurious lobby and addressed the front desk clerk wit' this attractive young man who stood behind it.

"He-llo." I said, accentuating my dazzling smile.

"Yes, ma'am, can I help you?" This coconut-skinned, lanky man wit' wavy blonde hair and a whiting smile spoke wit' such enthusiasm like he loveded his job.

"Yes, yes, I made a reservation to stay at your lovely hotel. The name is Ms. Khocolate wit' a 'K' but the credit card is under my fiancé's name. Could you please check it fo me?"

"Do you have the card number? It will be easier to find?" he axed.

"Oh, yes, it's…."

"Yes, Mr. Guy. Ma'am, your room number is 754. He hasn't arrived as of yet. Here is your key and you have a wonderful stay." The man concluded wit' an endearing smile.

"Thank you."

As I walked away I put some oomph in my strut jus' like that big chick in um…um *Waiting to Exhale*. That's right. I shook what my momma gave me. I knew that young man was checking me out wit'out even looking back. I was *finne*. Smelled it. Felt it. And mostly, I knew it.

As I stood in front of door 754, I sighed. It was a quick meditation fo me. Then I unlocked the door and stepped into paradise. Damn. My eyes lit up as I marveled the suite. Tall windows draped wit' beautiful curtains, polished Italian furniture, Oriental rug, accentuated wall-to-wall plush carpet, big, tall vases wit' fresh flowers, big screen television wit' CD and DVD. The bedroom was exquisite. Big king-sized bed wit' Ralph Lauren bedding, fluffy pillows and pillow shams, mahogany wood nightstands and dresser wit' antique lamps and the Jacuzzi in its separate space off to the living room. Exquisite.

I rolled my eyes and sucked my teeth. I was pissed! That room shoulda been mines. And I knew I had to work the hell outta Mr. Guy to get my shit!

Fo some reason, I got angry at the fact that I was livin' in the freakin' projects when I envisioned myself basking in that room. I knew that I had to pump my coochie, tease, please, suck, and fuck the shit outta Mr. Guy. I wanted to get paid fo my pretty perfume pussy. And the next time I stepped foot into paradise it would be my own muthafucking house.

I got undressed, opened my traveling bag and pulled out a hot pink thong. That was it. My titties were perky. It gave me a boost of confidence as I felt it would give Mr. Guy something to gawk at. Reel him in quickly. Time was muthafuckin' money.

I soaked in the Jacuzzi fo twenty minutes and then I heard the door jiggle. Semi-sweet red wine was chilling in the ice bucket. The lights were dimmed. Robin Thicke softly played. Black rose petals made a path to the bed and on his pillow laid a piece of chocolate covered cherry. Once he bit into it, it would be like having me. Yes, an oozing orgasm. *Mmmmmmmmmgood.*

Incoming stepped this tall, distinguished looking man wit' tanned skin, and a wary look upon his face. He was attractive. *Think God*, I thought. I had had some pitiful looking puppies in my day. Mr. Guy being attractive was an added bonus fo me because I could actually get aroused by him. I wouldn't have to fake it.

"Hello. Would you mind pouring us a drink?" I axed flirting wit' my eyes.

He seemed startled, but tried to play it off.

"No, no, not at all." He made hand gestures as he fumbled wit' the flute glasses nearly breaking one. But his quick reflexcs caught it before it hit the floor. That raised my left brow. I found Mr. Guy interesting.

Mr. Guy poured us two glasses of wine and walked over to hand it to me. Then he lowered his head.

"Are you okay?" I axed wit' a sincere tone in my voice.

He scratched his throat and stretched his starched neck collar to his dress shirt, as his eyes wandered around the luxurious suite until they finally planted onto my bare skin.

"Yes. I must admit I'm a bit uncomfortable." he said.

"I understand." I nodded my head and stared into his

eyes, took a sip of wine and then I set the flute glass down and emerged from the waters anticipating him to gaze at my sheer beauty.

I stood up as my raisin-colored nipples poked out. His green eyes widened and then lowered as I witnessed a bulge protruding in his pants. I smirked. It didn't take long fo me to see that Mr. Guy had indeed been starvin' and I needed to feed him plenty to get my muthafucken house.

My movement was slow as a snail. One hand palmed my tit as the other inched its way down to my thong and eased it down my legs so seductively.

Mr. Guy's mouth watered.

He stared down my every movement until I was now face-to-face wit' him in the nude. I ran my fingers through his brunette hair. Close up he resembled Clark Kent. Ooh, I usedta to have the biggest crush on Superman. I nibbled on his fuzzy ear, pecked his long neck, and my warm hand touched the back of his dress shirt to calm his anxiety. He could feel that I was on fire.

I unbuttoned his Brooks Brothers dress shirt and he wiggled it off his shoulders as it fell to the crease of his elbows. Then he slowly pulled it off. I raised his arms and took off his v-neck T-shirt, and unzipped his trousers as they dropped down to his fine leather shoes.

I kneeled down exposing the crack of my flawless ass as I untied his laces and had him sit down so that I could slip off one shoe at a time, followed by his pants. There he sat in jus' his boxers wit' a huge bulge standing tall. My long fingers slithered into the slit and pulled out his tan dick. It was plump like a Ball Park. I then tilted my head and permitted my tongue to lick, lick, lick, around, around, around wit' saliva drooling from my mouth and scooping it backup, up, up, up, and sliming it down, down, down, down, until I swallowed him whole tasting his manhood in one sultry bite. Mr. Guy's eyelids closed and his tongue massaged his thin lips. He leaned back and let me pleasure him. His left hand caressed my slender neck, as his right hand caressed my left tit. I moaned. It had been some time since I had actually felt that way. The imagery of fucking Clark Kent might have had something to do wit' it.

I took Mr. Guy by the hand and we traveled the road to paradise as I laid him onto the bed and devoured his manhood like I hadn't eaten in days. I slithered up his body and sucked on his rock hard, pinkish-colored nipples, and then stood on all fours and wiggled to feel my hole on his brick hard dick, and slithered down the pole, screwing him like the cap on a twist bottle.

Up and down, down and up, wit' pussy juice gushing out of me. My G-spot was overflowing wit' lust.

I rotated my body with my juicy ass facing him as I rode him into the sunset, slow and sensually making my potent pussy softly murmur. Mr. Guy couldn't take the pleasures as he moaned loudly, temples bursting through his tanned skin, eyes clasped in darkness as his fingers gripped the sheets and his toes stood erect slowly curling under in ecstasy.

Then, came the final finale as he bellowed while quivering full of exhilaration, "I'm coooom-ing, Pink Khocolate!!!!" I watched his eyes roll in the back of his head, body shivering the pleasures as I glanced at my Movado watch thinking he gave me a run fo my damn money. Shit.

I was truly famished fo that house that I worked past my two-hour shift. Regardless, I got paid wit' a parting tip. Smack dab in my hands Mr. Guy placed fifteen hundred dollars and I was droppin' it like it was hot in my fine ass skin. *Ka-Ching!*

Normally, I wouldn't see a client twice, but I woulda

made an exception fo Mr. Guy. It was something about him resembling Clark Kent that really got my coochie sloppy wet. *Mmmmmmmmmm.*

I dropped my wheels off at the garage and caught a taxi home. I was tired as hell and I knew Bedell shoulda been sound asleep. It was 4:00 a.m. I placed a hundred and fifty dollars on the kitchen table fo when Bedell woke up. 'Ey, I had her thinking I was working part-time at some retail store in the mall as a sales associate and as a part-time hostess at a 24-hour diner, so I had to keep the lie going. And plus, if I woulda given Bedell more money she might've gotten suspicious. Probably thought I was out selling drugs or something. What was I 'sposed to say? "Ma, I'm out selling pussy." There was no way I was gonna tell her that.

Bedell knew nuthin' about designer wear and if she did happened to see something on TV, wit' me working at the mall she knew damn well I couldn't afford it. I had to be rockin' bootleg. Yeah, she woulda thought bootleg.

As fo the second job I told her it balanced my funds out so that I could help her out as well as keep some loot in my pockets. I had to work. I was try'na to do right by her. Wit' Bedell working two jobs, she barely had time fo herself let alone time to worry about me. As long as that money was hitting that table every week…muthafucka was the word.

I stepped into my bedroom, shut the door, and got undressed and then plopped on the bed and crashed until morning, which actually was noon.

When I awoke it was 1:00 p.m. and I was groggy as hell. I crawled to the foot of the bed and reached fo my traveling bag and unzipped it. I pulled out $1350.00. I sat up and stood to walk into my closet and reached up to the top shelf and grabbed my silver box wit' key. I unlocked it and pulled out the rest of my money and sat there and counted it all. I separated it in denominations of: 1s, 5s, 10s, 20s, 50s, 100s, and rubber band them all and jotted down $5000.00 on a piece of Post-it and attached it under one of the rubber bands and tucked the money back in its box, locked it, and put it back on the top shelf in the closet.

I lay back against the pillows feeling like 5Gs was pretty damned good fo all the clients I'd had. Pretty damned.

I heard my stomach growl so I rose to my feet and walked into the bathroom to freshen up. Then I stepped out into the living room thinking I was home alone but to my surprise Bedell was sitting at the kitchen table wit' a cup of coffee in one hand and a newspaper in the other. The money was still lying on the table.

"Good mornin', momma."

"Morning chile, it's the afternoon. You jus' gonna sleep your life away."

"Momma, I am tired from working. You forget I do have two jobs."

"Oh, I know baby." She sighed, this hopeless sigh that stopped me in my tracks as my right bare foot overlapped my left and my back leaned against the second-hand Kitchen-Aid refrigerator that hummed all times of the night.

"Momma, what's wrong?" I axed, as I looked at her, a face of thinness, yet skin that was firm. Her hair had grassroots of gray strands scattered all over her head. She looked frail, sleep deprived wit' discolored bags under her eyes. She looked worn.

"Oh, don't worry yourself, honey." Bedell waved her hand. She tried to change the subject by saying, "Pretty-Boy called collect this mornin' says he comin' home in 2010. Promise me, Embellish that you won't get caught up in those drugs, please?" She rubbed her chin as her root-beer-colored eyes locked wit' a gloss of burdened cast over them.

"I promise, momma." I lowered my head fo about a second. "Momma talks to me?"

Bedell massaged her face as she often did when she was stressing. "I got laid off from my second job. We got bills." She quickly balled up a fist and placed it at her mouth feeling as though that shouldn't have slipped out.

I walked over and sat down at the kitchen table.

I took her hands and placed them in mine, "Momma, don't worry we will get through this. I'll jus' put in some extra hours, okay."

Bedell eyes widened wit' such gratitude. "How'd you grow up so fast, huh, Embellish?" She axed in a soft tone.

I stared dead-eyed into space. I turned staring at my bedroom door and then turned my head back and looked momma in her face, "I dunno, Momma. I dunno."

Bedell's frail hand caressed my face so motherly that I felt like I wanted to lay my head in her bosom and cry a much-needed cry. But I couldn't. The tears would not flow. I literally felt dead inside. But something deep wit'in was pushing me to tell momma the truth.

I took a deep breath and looked momma dead in her eyes and I said, "Momma, he hurt me."

Her forehead wrinkled and her eyes drooped.

"Who hurt you?" she axed.

"Pretty-Boy."

She waved her frail hand. "Oh, Embellish, kids play all the time."

"No, Momma, he hurt me by having sex wit' me. I was eleven, Momma."

Momma flung her arms to push me off of her as if I

was contagious or something. Then she stood and sassed talked me wit' a stern look on her face. "Now, Embellish, I don't tolerate no lying in my house. Just...just stop that nonsense, you hear me! You stop that foolish talk! Your brother loves you. He would never do such a thing. Never! Not my chile, no siree."

I looked at momma wit' the straightness of face and I said, "Yes, Momma. I'm sorry fo lying in your home. It will never happen again."

I rose to my feet and walked into my bedroom and stared out of my bedroom window feeling like a dagger had been stabbed in my heart. It was the worst feeling in the world. I swept my *dirt* under the rug and left it there. I felt as though if Momma didn't believe me who else would.

***

Desperate times called fo desperate measures and I knew I had to up my game. The last thang I wanted was to see momma worrying herself sick. I felt that I could still get my house and help her wit' the bills. I wanted to ease some stress offa her. Nah. I didn't wanna see momma die over some damn bills. I woulda gladly taken on the worry and taken my frustrations out on my clients. The harder I worked, the more money I would make. I just had to think smarter.

Instead of my tiny ad in Play Thang, an adult toy magazine. I decided to bid a little higher and placed an ad in Blow. I had heard that many businessmen skim through those pages seeking to find something new and naughty. Well, I knew I was as naughty and as new as they'd come. I had raised my standards. I wasn't willing to just fuck anybody. Nah. You had to come wit' something: brains, stamina, good credit, be a professional businessman like former Governor of New York, Eliot Spitzer (who woulda thought that *he* woulda been so supportive of the power of the pussy. Bless you Spitzer!), and most importantly the cash. Hmmm. Shit, those high-class pussies were making some serious, serious loot.

Anyways, if you were *fine* that was an added bonus fo me. I learned a lot from back in the day when I was practically giving my pussy away fo *free*. Those days were over. I was hopeful that someone would see the ad and give a sista a hollah—very hopeful.

I got dressed around 3:00 p.m. and had gone outside to inhale some pollution as I stood in front of Broke-Down Housing jus' taking in the surroundings. All I saw was debris, broken glass, graffiti bulletproof windows, a couple of rookies walking the beat, and jailbait pushing baby strollers. I rolled my eyes and crossed my arms about my chest and shook my head. Most of the junkies were black running around hopelessly lost. It made my stomach churn.

As I blinked them out I thought about where I would want to live to get away from all that was painted before me.

I remembered when I took a drive through Franklin Lakes, New Jersey. Actually I got lost try'na find Glenrock. I missed my turn and I got pissed, but after seeing how the other half liveded I mellowed out. Man, I could see myself living among the uppity whites. Shit...I felt that I would fit right in. Those houses looked like fuckin' mansions. No litter. No noise. Just road kill; darkness 'cause there damn sho' ain't much lighting and the air reminded me of being Down South. I knew that I could have it all. I jus' had to be a lil' mo' patient.

The day was rather dead so I resumed back to my

roach motel hoping my phone would ring. I needed to get at least two more clients before the week was out.

About 8:00 p.m. my Pink BlackBerry wailed.

"Hel-lo. What's your pleasure?" I sat up in the closet wit' the door shut and hid between my Burberry and Armani dresses staring at the price tags.

"Mucho gusto. Si, me llamo Fehrnahndoh."

(A pleasure. Yes, my name is Fernando.)

"Si. Yo hablo mal el espanol." I said.

(Yes. I speak Spanish badly.)

"Por el contrario, lo habla muy bien!" He said.

(On the contrary, you speak it very well!)

"Que hace usted?" I axed.

(What do you do?)

"El abogado."

(Lawyer.)

"Si, Cargar el cuarto." I said

(Yes, to charge the room.)

"Si, Tarjta de credito."

(Yes, credit card.)

"Si." I said.

(Yes.)

"Favor de repetirlo?" I axed.

(Repeat it, please?)

"Si." He said.

(Yes.)

I was gettin' exhausted talking to this dude. *Man, speak goddamn English, shit!* I had to take some short cuts wit' him so I could get his credit card number. As we were talking I was keying it in to make the reservations at the West Mansion Hotel in SoHo, New York. We were set to meet around ten so I had time to lounge around and chill fo about a half hour before I had to get all glittered up fo a night of Spanish passion.

I laid out my Nicole Miller "little black dress" and my Stella McCartney pumps. I took a shower around

8:45 and made myself fabulous-looking. I wanted him to be stunned by my natural beauty. Some men's I didn't have to over-dramatize. Some men's actually enjoyed a simplistic woman. And that was what Fernando was gettin' wit' a sweet scent of "Lovely" to stimulate his libido.

I grabbed my Prada bag, traveling bag, and headed out the door.

I took the #22 bus that my new acquaintance, Boulevard Thrillman drove to Raymond Street. I walked a block to Mr. Rays Garage and to my surprise Mr. Rays was there.

"Hello. Embellish, you know I've been meaning to talk to you." Mr. Rays stared me down wit' those hard eyes.

I strike a pose leaning on one leg. "Oh...what 'bout?"

"You know I've been more than generous with you, wouldn't you say?"

I paused fo a brief second, "Well, um, yeah."

"So do you think I've been treated fairly?" He took two steps forward in his dirty overalls, sucked his teeth, as his eyes devoured me.

"Well, um, yes. I think I have been more than fair. I keep my space clean and I cater to you."

"Do you really cater to me? I mean when was the last time you really, really catered to me, huh?"

He had me there.

"Well, prices are rising so I'm gonna have to start charging you for your space unless—"

I knew where he was headed and I didn't like it one bit. Mr. Rays put a little snag in my plan when he told me that he was thinking about charging me to keep my car in his garage. I thought quickly on my feet because that would be an expense I couldn't afford to pay wit' Bedell losing her second job.

I lured Mr. Rays in and kneeled on my knees and slopped him up like honey on a biscuit and all was forgotten.

I hopped in Pleasure-Me-Down and drove off wit' a nasty taste in my mouth. I felt like I had cat hair stuck in my throat from his fuzzy balls. *Yuck!* Obviously, Mr. Rays hadn't washed his balls in a coupla days. Shit!

I arrived at the West Mansion Hotel at 10:47 p.m. I was late. Blame it on traffic. But before exiting out of the car I slipped a peppermint Altoid in my mouth, popped the trunk fo my traveling bag, exited, grabbed it and headed fo the lobby.

I confirmed my reservation wit' this dirty blond, anorexic, ghostly looking woman who scared me half to death when she opened her mouth. *Haven't you visited a dentist lately?* Boy was it on the tip of my tongue. The dirty blond woman confirmed my reservation under Fernando Vasquez. She handed me a key fo room 256 and I made my way to the elevator.

Once on the floor and in front of the door, I took a moment to meditate before unlocking the door. I stepped in and the suite was of utter beauty. Oh, it was betta' than the one at the Wilton Hotel. Everything was upscale. And I instantly found myself boiling inside jus' as before. *Why do I have to live like a hood rat!* I distracted my thoughts wit' why I was there: to make my loot. So I got into character. Opened my traveling bag and pulled out a black ruffled thong, whip, and my hoochie stiletto boots that rose up to my kneecaps wit' no bra. I massaged some shine to my scalp so it wouldn't look dull. I looked like a vixen. The baddest bitch in town.

As I was finishing up I heard a noise coming from the bedroom. And their soaking in the Jacuzzi was Fernando sipping on a glass of Remy Martin Champagne Cognac.

"Hello, madam Khocolate, would you care for a glass?"

My eyes widened. "Wait a minute. You know how to speak English...then why?"

He blushed. "I have to be careful just as you."

Okay, he's shrewd. A bad boy. My lips protruded *ooh!*

I cut my eyes slightly and made my way down from his dark black locks, to the nape of his tree trunk neck. I sashayed my way to the front of him as I gaped at his debonair features that made my insides hot. His dark eyes, broad nose, and his delicious come-and-get-me-lips made my body pulsate. Fernando was wet all over, too. Dammmmmnnnnnnn, everything looked right from the head down to his perfectly defined chest. I just hoped, rather prayed that the package down below was of equal pleasure 'cause if so, it would be on and pussy pop-pop-poppin'!

Fernando was yummy to look at.

I sashayed my sexy signature walk and circled him, never taking my eyes off of him. Fernando made me hungry. He had that confident demeanor. Ooh, it was a turn on.

He rose out of the water and his shriveled taupe-colored dick stared at me. I was minutely disappointed in the lil' fellah, but as Fernando stood in front of me, his blood brother raised its tired head and BANG! That gun was loaded ready to ravage my pussy.

Fernando grabbed me manly around my curvaceous waist and kissed me passionately like he had missed me something awful. My head spun jus' a little. Then, he led me to the oval bed and gently pushed me as I fell back onto a cushion of softness. His aggressiveness turned me on even more. Fernando's eyes zoomed in as he parted my legs and leaned down to kiss my cat. The lil' head purred. He teased its pinkish tongue wit' his long luscious tongue and sucked it so endearingly. "Ooh, it feels sooooooo good." I sung. The wetness was oozing out of me as Fernando slurped my coochie juice. His tongue made me shiver. I was on *Fuego* (fire)! He sucked me longingly as my eyes fluttered, and then he turned me on all fours and teased and licked my asshole like he was *sed* (thirsty). Aaahhhhhhhh," I moaned and bit down on my lips as his dick entered its tight cavity.

I gritted and grinded my teeth as his hard strokes aroused inward and outward. He rotated his dick so skillfully in my ass *Aprisa* (quickly), *Despacio* (slowly), as I clawed at the immaculate bedding. "Dammit!" I bellowed in a sensual tone. The bed squeaked fo mercy as I maneuvered my glistening body and rode him like a ghetto-chick high offa crack. I was gettin' tired as hell.

Fernando's eyes remained closed as I rotated my apple ass and faced him. I squatted and pumped him hard. My head was sweating profusely, titties flapped against my ribcage and my ass cheeks clapped against his skin wit' beads of wetness streaming down the crack.

"HARDER!" Fernando demanded while smacking my ass, pPOP, pPOP, pPOP!

Ooh, Ooh, Ooh…I pumped him so hard that I felt his dick ooze cum inside of my ass as his body shuddered and he gained a cramp in his legs. It was the best sex I had had in years. Fernando and I was a match made in heaven. Knowing that I knew that I could not see him again. That was part of my policy. And if he wanted to see the fine print to my contract I would jus' lay back, open my legs wide, and have him read my lips:

"Due to the high demand of my juicy pussy please read my lips carefully: one fuck, per dick."

I raised my drenched body and grabbed the bottle of Remy and took it to the head. Fernando eyes widened to my unladylike display, but I was thirsty as hell. He leaned his head back and chuckled.

"Madam Khocolate, you are full of surprises." He grabbed his satchel and pulled out some money and looked at me lustfully as I kept on nursing that bottle.

"Madam Khocolate, I would like to see you again."

I stopped and pulled the bottle from my lips.

"Fernando, that won't be possible. I don't make it a habit of seeing my clients twice."

"Oh, but I will make it worth your while." He smirked confidently.

"How?"

"Well, I am willing to offer you four thousand dollars, today, if you are willing to be at my beck and call always. That means wherever and whenever I call you you drop everything to be where I say."

"Four thousand, huh?" I cut my eyes to the ceiling.

"Si, four thousand." He swayed the money in his hands and cut his eyes over at me. "I am a man of my word, Madam Khocolate."

I turned my back to think things over. Seconds later my phone rang. "Excuse me." I said, and made my way into the living room to answer it.

I pulled out my Pink BlackBerry from my Prada bag and tilted my head to the side and spoke in my seductive tone.

"Hel-lo. What's your pleasure?"

"*I want some pussy.*" The vulgar man said.

"Who is this?" I axed, a little surprised by his straightforwardness.

"Four thousand."

I turned around and Fernando was standing in the doorway wit' his rock hard dick and his finger inching me to c'mere.

I closed the face to the phone and took a deep breath fo round two. It was gonna be a long night.

After, I walked out of the West Mansion Hotel like I was bowlegged. Fernando put a hurtin' on my pussy and ass. I entered the car like an old lady and drove off and stopped at the nearest Duane Reade fo some Epsom salt. My pussy was sore as hell, but it was worth four thousand.

I started counting in my head. I had nine thousand all together. A ghetto bitch was gettin' paid like that.

When I arrived home I had no choice but to soak my ass in that dingy bathtub. I damn near squatted before relaxing in the soothing hot water. My mind drifted as I closed my eyes dreaming about where I wanted to be, how I wanted to be living wit' all of my fancy shit. I felt I deserved more than the projects and I was going to get it. My conscience was content wit' what I was doing 'cause I felt it was foa good cause. Me. I was worth so much and I was not gonna deny myself the pleasures of happiness.

After my bath, I took it down a notch and got some sleep. Sista was tired as hell.

***

I was catching the bus rather frequently to take care of business. I hadn't seen Boulevard Thrillman in a while. Normally, he would drive the #22 bus if I went to Mr. Rays Garage. I always thought he was a cutie. Mainly his eyes were his sexiest assets. He had those doe-eyes. Eyes that burnt through me and made me feel all squishy inside. I felt like he was trying to heal me from the inside out as he gazed at me.

Finally, I did see him when I rode the bus. I paid the fare and we'd engage in small talk. Actually, around that time I started going back to *church*, not regularly, but on occasion, and he would be driving on those particular Sundays.

He'd smile.

I'd smile.

And that was as far as it would go. I was still running game, but I was also try'na find God as well as myself. My body was getting tired. I wanted a change in careers. Do something worthwhile, you know. Make good of my life—myself.

When I looked at Boulevard he seemed like a fresh start. I usedta watch him and he was always pleasant to his patrons. He seemed in good spirits on the outside. I didn't know him that good but something was drawing me closer towards him wit'out his knowledge. I wanted to get to know him while gettin' to know me.

Boulevard knew nuthin' about my life 'cause I was very evasive. Thereafter, I started bumping into him in the streets, mostly on Playa Ave at Kutt-da-Bullshit, a barbershop I frequented.

My barber, Holey would hook a sista's 'do up. And all those thugged-out bitches would be hatin' and sweating me. Don't get it twisted I was not a carpet licker, okkkkkkkkkkkkkkkk.

Well, to my surprise Boulevard frequented the same barbershop. I dug his look, his tone, and his laugh jus' made him sexier to me. He was special fine.

The outer of Boulevard was everythang I could imagine having in between my legs, but I didn't know his inner and I was not try'na find out. Even though I was digging him I had to put him on pause. I had a lot of work to do on me.

Gradually, I started seeing Boulevard more and

more. And again, we would engage in small talk and that was it. I was going through so much. I needed a friend—someone who didn't know me or of my history—someone who would listen to me, someone who would care 'bout me. We had finally exchanged numbers and I had given him a call while I was at the Laundromat. It felt good to talk to someone new. I was very upfront about "finding me" wit'out going into explicit detail. I told Boulevard. "Look, I gotta lotta shit on my plate. My life is complicated." Deep down I wanted to expose myself to him. Free myself, but I didn't trust him enough.

"You're not happy. I don't know your situation, but all I can say is why be in something if you're not happy. Why waste your precious time?"

"It's complicated like I said, Boulevard."

"I hears yah, but it's up to you to change that, Ma."

"Look, I have nuthin' to offer you, at this present time." I said, wit' a frown on my face.

"But what do you have to offer yourself, Ma?"

I lowered my head while on the payphone. After hanging up I dried and folded my clothes, yet I kept his words in my head.

I walked home in a daze. Boulevard's words pierced my heart deeper than I could ever imagine. I felt like I wanted to breakdown and cry. But I didn't. I couldn't. Boulevard's words had me thinking about my situation—my lifestyle. Fo some reason, it was starting to bother me on so many levels. I knew that if it was meant to be wit' Boulevard or anyone else I had to work on me. I hoped that I would one day see Boulevard again, but this time in the company of my own home. All I could do was dream.

When arrived home I sat in my bedroom and listened to my CD "The Miseducation Of Lauryn Hill," and I thought hard about finding my own destiny. And finally things started to manifest.

My situation had improved tremendously. Wit' the nine thousand I had I invested in a small two-level condo in Bloomfield, New Jersey, fo Bedell and me. But Bedell didn't want to leave her nest. She told me to spread my wings 'cause I had always been there when she needed me. I couldn't stand to see her livin' in the projects but she said that she had put in fo Section-8 and she was waiting fo her approval letter to come in the mail. I thought it was a waste of time, but who was I to stomp on my momma's beliefs.

"Momma, if you change your mind my door is always open to you."

"Oh baby, I know. You're such a loving chile. I am so proud of you, Embellish."

Tears flooded my eyes fo the first time 'cause of momma's words. I had a breakthrough that I never saw coming.

I made my home as comfy and cozy as I could. I had no visitors. I needed to be in solitude to search fo me 'cause I was truly lost. I yearned fo someone positive in my life. Not someone who would take my kindness fo its weakness and manipulate to get what he wanted. I worked my ass off and God had blessed me wit' a home, in spite of how I made my money. It might not have been the home in Franklin Lakes, New Jersey, but it was a ways from the 'hood. It was a stepping-stone fo me to move forward. I had my own space and privacy. There were no rodents. No roaches. No junkies, prostitutes, hustlers, thugs or little gurls pushing baby strollers pretending to be grown wearing Daisy dukes wit' their ass cheeks hanging out and halter tops calling themselves single mommies. The young ladies I saw

50

pushing baby strollers looked dignified. There were no syringes in the hallway. No piss reeking. No grungy and dirty bathroom. Everythang was clean. The neighborhood was quiet and my neighbors were neighborly. This was a whole new beginning fo me.

Things were changing in my life. I became a regular at Serenity Missionary Baptist Church around the corner from my house. I stopped spending a lot of money on designer wear and started giving my tithes and offerings to the church. I stopped hoeing around to make my loot. I actually got a real job working at a beauty salon called Evolve, as a receptionist. Yeah, as much as I stayed on the phone I had many years of experience. And I had also enrolled in Diva's Beauty Academy at night fo Cosmetology. Something I always desired to do. I was changing my life around fo the betta'. But thoughts would run through my mind when money got tight. I'd find myself backsliding from church. The old habits were creeping back. The Pink BlackBerry was being pulled out of its hiding place and the "Khocolate Companion" was dying to come out and play. Money was always my weakness. I felt like I was fighting wit' the devil. I kept clinging to the old way and hurting more and more each time.

One day I turned on the Pink BlackBerry and I listened to all the clients who were try'na contact me fo a evening of pleasuring. I grinned 'cause I was not forgotten. Fernando was the main client calling like he was famished fo my perfume pussy. I was tempted to return his call, but my fingers would not entertain the thought. Deep inside I wanted to but once I looked around at the progress I was making wit'out lying on my back I actually felt good about myself fo the first time in my entire life. *So what I'm broke*, I thought.

Eventually the Pink BlackBerry hid back in its hiding place and I continued to move forward. I grew tired and around that time was when I saw Boulevard again. I knew I wanted and needed to taste something new, fresh and easygoing. I had enough of old, stale and miserable. I needed to give my mind, body, and soul a break.

***

November 13, 3:30 P.M.

Boulevard and I talked fo a half hour on the phone.

"If a woman can give me the two "ffs" I will be hers for life." He said.

I had a delayed reaction. "OK, I get it, "feed/fuck." I laughed out loud.

Before going to work Boulevard said that he would stop by.

"Okay." I said.

I was off that day, but I had a meeting to go to later at the job. Some big shot was coming to the salon to market his products.

"Can a brotha' gets some lunch?" He asked jokingly.

"Do you want anything 'pecific?"

I knew how to burn in the kitchen even though I did my best work in the bedroom.

"No."

"Okay, I can whip up something." I said, and gave him directions to my house.

During our conversation Boulevard was laying it on thick about how he got down. *Shhh...I'd rather you show me when the time is right*, I thought. Talk was cheap. I had plenty of men's who used that gift of gab and I didn't want another one. Boulevard kept on running off at the mouth and I remained quiet smirking on the inside.

Tsk, tsk, tsk, I swayed my index finger. *He'll learn,* I thought.

By the time, Boulevard arrived his lunch, a hot pastrami wit' Swiss cheese on rye bread complimented by some Dijon mustard was ready. I was nervous as hell 'cause I had a "man" coming to my house—a *new* man. 'Ey, it wasn't like I had every Pedro, Mario, and Marcus at my place. This was a big deal fo me. This dating stuff was all new to me. And it showed. Boulevard saw that I was rather uncomfortable, but he tried his best to calm my nerves by taking my hand and massaging it.

I gave him the grand tour and had his food on the kitchen table. I left Boulevard in the kitchen by hisself so that he could eat. He slowly ate while I sat in the living room. Well, not sat I kept pacing the floor like a jackass. I was so nervous. I was try'na listen for that "Ahhhhhhhhh" sound. Shit, I needed to pass the feeding test 'cause I knew hands down the fucking test was a sho' win for me. I was a pro at that.

"This is good." Boulevard said.

"Thank you."

What a relief, I thought, *one down...one more to go.*

After Boulevard ate, he cleaned off his plate and washed his dish and came into the living room. I made room fo him on the black sofa. I blushed not believing that he was in my presence. *Damn, he's fine,* I thought. And he was tall too. I was delighted. It had been years fo this moment to arrive. Years! How often does that happen? Usually people move on and you never see them again. But I had spoken on this earlier and I guess God was listening. My life was in disarray before and I still had a lot of work to do to get back on track. But I realized that I could have a friend.

I glanced over at him as my head rested on the back of my hand and my elbow sunk into the cushion of the sofa. Boulevard turned and stared into my eyes wit' his gray hat snuggled on his head. I lent in and he lent in and our lips greeted our first official hello. We spoke wit' our tongues: "How you been?" tongues twirling wit' lust. "How was your day?" saliva smothering and forming miniature bubbles in our mouth. "How are you feeling?" wit' our eyes closed and our conversation long and engaging. We came to a concluding sentence as our lips parted. All I could think was, *Wow!* I knew that I wanted to get to know Boulevard betta'. Our attraction was strong.

2:20 A.M... November 14

It was touch and go wit' the phone calls. Boulevard was working and I was taking it down a notch from a hard days work at the salon. I could hear the cars zooming through the streets, sirens and red lights flashing through my curtains in the living room. I heard people walking, laughing as if it were 98 degrees outside. There was a chill in the air so I turned the thermostat up to 72.

I took a hot shower, lotion down my moist skin with some Curel Natural Healing as I inhaled its jasmine extracts. Mmmmm. I smelled quite lovely. I put on my white teddy and put Vaseline on my feet, washed my face and brushed my teeth before bed.

The phone rang.

"Hello."

"Yes."

"It's… Oh, you forgot. When? Okay."

Click.

I paced the floor wit' my titties jiggling. Breathe. It was too good to be true. Boulevard was stopping by, again. Breathe. I sniffed my skin to see if the fragrance had died. I scrunched up my nose. I peeked out of my mini-blinds to see if I saw him driving up in his black Acura RL. I glanced at the clock. I paced some more. I listened to the quiet outside. *It must be damn cold outside 'cause hardly anyone's out,* I thought. Oh, shit, it's two in the morning.

I could hear myself think unlike when I was living in Knock-Boots. I sniffed myself again, questioning if I had put deodorant on. Then I walked back into the bathroom, turned the nozzle, pulled off the layers, and stood under the showerhead and *Caress* myself down. I towel dried and slipped into something a bit more revealing and covered my sexy in my white bathrobe. I knew this was no social call. I felt it earlier in the day…the chemistry.

The phone rang.

"Yes."

"Ok."

"I'm coming."

"Push it open."

Lock. Lock. Lock. Lock.

"Have a seat."

"Would you like something to drank?"

Breathe.

I started pacing the floor again.

"C'mere."

I swallowed and stopped pacing while tugging on the belt of my robe as I walked over to him and stood in front of him as he sat on the sofa. He opened my robe and caressed my bare skin, shoulders, arms, breasts, thighs, and inched his way around to my ass. I knelt down, my head rested on his collarbone, inhaling his manly scent that drove me insane. My fingers cradled the back of his neck, tongued tasted his earlobe, and my lips (peck, peck, peck) his. Breathe.

He disrobed me out of my bathrobe as it dangled down and fell to the crease of my elbows. His hands sized my waist like a crab's claw. My head tilted back as I stared at the ceiling. My ears were eavesdropping to the outside world. It was quiet. Inside I heard the pipes clanking easing the heat up. I could smell it. His lips soothed my neck wit' gentleness. His hands cupped my titties and eased down to massage my ass, as I exhaled. He desired me up close and personal.

He rose to his feet, balancing me as he climbed the stairwell wit' care carrying me over the threshold into a world of titillation.

"I'm going to pleasure you." Boulevard said.

I thought I had died and gone to a resort fo deprived pussies. Lord knows I had an angel watching over me.

Boulevard laid me on the canopy bed and I could hear his navy blue pants drop to the floor. His layers: navy cardigan sweater, white collared shirt, black boots, and his cell phone rested on his clothes that he lay on the heated radiator to keep warm. The heat was seriously pumping and so was my heart. And then something so unexpected eased out of my mouth, "Please don't hurt me?" And I wasn't talking 'bout his love tool hurtin' me either. I was referring to his words that flowed into my ears like a rippling wave, slowly surfing on a roller coaster of high tides.

"Lay still. Let me pleasure you since you are always taking care of everyone else and not yourself." He said.

So I obliged.

He aroused me as I tried to tune the world out. But I couldn't. My mind was on speed dial almost spoiling my 3:00 in the morning dessert.

"You like that?" he axed in a whisper.

I raised my body wanting to join in, but he insisted, "No, let me pleasure you." It was pure torture fo me 'cause I was the queen of control. My opportunity had finally come and I couldn't participate. In my mind I was pulling hair I no longer had. Shit.

I heard "Magnum Twister" tear open. I knew the moment had arrived and I exhaled anticipating that moment fo over a year and a half. Spittle glossed my lips, anxious. Immediately, something felt limp. There was no hard-on protruding to be let in.

"I want to get hard inside of you." Boulevard said.

But...but shouldn't you already be hard as a rock? My mind kept on thinking...*If you don't have a girlfriend, aren't married, not living wit' a woman, don't have a piece on the side...shouldn't you be ravaging me right about now? Shouldn't you be filling out that condom? Why is it loose?* I swallowed those thoughts very slowly down to my stomach and let them absorb into the acid that had settled.

The heat was blazing. It was getting hot in there and not from the makings of fuckin'. Boulevard tried energetically, but his other half musta been out partying to the crack of dawn or something. I was glistening due to the humidity not 'cause of the workout that made me parched. Then it dawned on me. *Maybe he doesn't find me attractive 'cause I am not all dolled up. Maybe I don't excite him? Maybe...Maybe? Maybe? Maybe, he looks at me and sees a BOY 'cause of my low cut? Maybe, I am not enough "woman" for him?*

Sadly to say, the "Magnum" was highly disappointed as was I as was Boulevard.

"I am so embarrassed." He said. "I, I." His words stuttered fo a reasonable explanation.

To me it was what it was.

"Don't be embarrassed." I said.

Fo some reason his lack thereof didn't get me to the point whereas I wanted to reduce him down to a crumb wit' all that talking he was doing. Nah. Sometimes we put too much emphasis on one thing instead of focusing on the main thing. The main thing wit' Boulevard was that he made me feel special, regardless of his performance. His kisses, hugs, and cuddling meant more to me and did more for me than the act itself. Even if he had been Tarzan in the bedroom those essentials still woulda mattered more to me. I was changing in more ways than one. I was turning into a poetic soul of reason. Nevertheless, I was aroused by the thought of if there should be a next time it would most certainly be different. I tried to reassure him that, "'Ey, shit happens." It was no big deal. Women's go through shit all the time.

Boulevard took a shower while I laid across my bed in deep thought: *girlfriend, married, or some skank-hoe?* I had axed those questions prior and I had axed that evening and each time he said no to each one. Then why was my stomach feeling funny? I didn't know. It coulda been from my past experiences? Maybe from the mental and emotional and physical abuse I'd endured? Paranoia? Insecurity? Maybe my subconscious was fucking wit' me? I didn't know, but it bothered me. And I knew me enough to know that those questions would arise again.

Boulevard got dressed and laid across the bed. I couldn't sleep. Then around four o'clock his cell phone started blinking red. So I said, "Someone is calling you." Boulevard got up and checked his phone. And I got up and grabbed a pillow and blanket and had gone into the living room to lie down on the sofa: *girlfriend, married, or casual lover.* Eventually, he came into the living room and axed me to come back to bed.

"I have things on my mind. I prefer to lay here." I said.

"Well, let's talk about it."

I turned over and looked him in his eyes, "Was that a chick? Who else would be calling you this late?"

"That was my *boy.* He knows my schedule. Come back to bed?"

"It is the wee hours, Boulevard."

Boulevard stuck to his words and said, "He knows my schedule, baby."

I had gone back to bed, but I didn't get much sleep 'cause I felt I had been deceived. I was being faithful to Boulevard and I expected the same in return.

Girlfriend, Married, Casual Lover, Booty Caller, Old Flame, DL Brotha....

My list was growing by the minute.

11/14

Boulevard

[10:54:59 AM]

What's good s*exy?*

xxxENDxxx

When I first saw that text message my first initial thought was, *Yeah, right. Won't he stop playing wit' my mind 'cause he knows damn well I ain't sexy?*

After the wear and tear on my body I really looked down on myself. Sexy was no longer a part of my vocabulary. But I was flattered by his words. It broke me out into smiles. I couldn't remember the last time I even felt *sexy* let alone had someone say he thought I was. I had mixed emotions, but yet, I couldn't stop smiling. Boulevard made me feel good inside and he opened me up to something new. Something I hadn't done in a while—smile. But I had somehow changed that good feeling into something bad. *There was nuthin' fo me to be smiling about*, I thought. I had to look at the flipped side of thangs. I had moved into my own place. I had a job to support the household. My condo was decent. My mortgage was affordable. I was making major strides to betta' myself. Everythang I said I would do, I did. But during that time I couldn't remember if I smiled during the times I was getting my stroke on. I was taking care of business, but I wasn't stopping to look in the mirror and see *me*. The young woman who liveded in such agony, yet continued to open her legs. The young woman that tried to shade her past by sleeping wit' men's, men's she didn't even know. Yes, the woman whose faith had been compromised wit' layers and layers and layers of pain so she fucked her troubles away. I kept reverting backwards and I wasn't even aware of it. I thought I was livin' the life 'cause I had nice clothes, a hot ride, and money stashed away. But those materialistic things couldn't bring me *happiness*. I had to get lotta junk out of my head, heart, the crack of my ass, and layer one coat of spray paint over the graffiti art that was inscribed across the walls of my pussy. A reminder of all the men's I had fucked. I needed a serious, serious makeover.

I'm open, ready, and willing to smile again, I thought to myself.

I had to literally speak and feel that one sentence in order fo it to become my reality. I had to believe that someone would want to see me happy, besides, me. I had to convince myself that all men's weren't bad. I had to believe that there were some *gentle* men's out there. That I could be kissed, cuddled, and admired fo being myself, not some fantasy that was groped, fondled, and fucked up the ass. But I had to feel that I was *worthy* of such a man. I had to tooken out the trash, which was *me* and dump it in the garbage can and leave it. And I had to take a chance on someone new. And I had hoped that he wouldn't hurt me. I wasn't looking fo nobody. I was just try'na find me. It was most discouraging 'cause I had to rummage through my past pains to get to the core of my soul.

After the text message, I picked up the phone and called Boulevard. Damn, jus' hearing his mellow voice had me cheesing. I felt like an schoolgurl wit' the biggest crush on that brotha'. I felt revitalized, if only fo that moment. It certainly was a start from where I was—broken.

I was a battered soul try'na heal, but I couldn't do it alone. I talked to God and axed that He watch over me. I had lotta rebuilding to do. And having another man in my life was not on my agenda. I yearned fo a friend. I needed laughter in my life and Boulevard gave me that. He put me at ease. I felt he wouldn't purposely hurt me, maybe my feelings 'cause he talked that "real talk" but it was okay 'cause I was the same way.

When I was a little gurl I always tried being the *nice* gurl. The wholesome gurl, but *he* stole that innocence from me. So I looked at nice gurls as failures. They finished last in my book. And they got *hurt* the most. I was tired of finishing last and hurting. I was tired of not having a meaningful relationship and feeling empty. I wanted more. I wanted spontaneity in my life. I wanted intellectual conversations. I wanted fun. I wanted intimacy, not hard sex. I wanted peace and quiet. I wanted compliments. Showers together. Pecks and French kisses and long hugs. I wanted flowers and candy. And "just 'cause" gifts. I wanted to smell his scent hours after he had left my home. I wanted deep like, not love. I was not ready fo love. I didn't know what love was. I had never really experienced true love, 'cept for wit' Tyler. But looking back I considered that to be puppy love. That was my first admittance to changing my mindset. *Would I ever experience true love?* I would have to be open to it. But fo that moment of my life I wasn't thanking about true love. Who I was thanking about was Boulevard.

11/16

"Hi." I said.

"Um, can you call me back a lil' later?" Boulevard axed.

"Sure."

We hung up so I decided to go to the Laundromat.

10:00

"What's good?"

"Just watching TV."

My mind reverted back to: *Girlfriend, Married, Live-in-hoochie.*

"Um, can I ax you a question?"

"Go ahead."

"Um, how come you only call me while you're driving the bus or on yo way to somewhere? I'm sayin'…I notice this pattern wit' you. Is there someone or something I should know about?"

Frustration erupted from Boulevard.

"LOOK…I told you already! If you don't believe me that's on you, it's you, not me!" He snapped.

Where is all the tension coming from?

"Me! I am not involved with anyone!"

I didn't bother to interrupt him. I let him have his say.

"Yo', why were you so nervous that night I was at your house, huh? What you thought one of your niggas was comin' to tap yo coochie. Yeah, they fucked your head up! I could tell you been through some rough shit. Look, Ma, I don't need this shit! You know, you need to take a step back and work on you!"

Tears began to roll down my face 'cause I was nervous 'cause it was something new for me. It had nuthin' to do wit' another man. And I knew my head was fucked up from all the shit that was inflicted upon me, as well as the shit I inflicted upon myself. Boulevard broke me open and made me cry 'cause I knew I had a lotta work to do if I ever wanted a healthy relationship wit' a man.

I let the tears fall one by one fo all the shit I put myself through fo a measly piece of: DICK. I took the cocky tone from Boulevard and my backbone cracked back into proper perspective.

FUCK him!

11/20
Boulevard
[11:04:55 AM]
What's good baby? How's it going?
xxxENDxxx

I smiled.

Why are we bumping heads? Why is he a hothead? Why do he keep throwing old shit up in my face? I'm not seeing anyone. I'm try'na forget. I'm try'na move forward. I don't wanna spend my time bringing up old hurts. I'm try'na forget about all the dickheads, the dick, and how it made me feel. Why can't he understand that? I feel like I'm drowning.

Here I am try'na LOVE me the best way I know how. I am willing to do the work. Try'na regain back what I had lost...me. But I can't grow if he constantly keeps throwing old pain in my face. How can I grow? How can I move forward into the arms of LOVE? How?

I mean Boulevard can be smooth and delicious in my presence, but over the phone he leaves a bad taste in my

63

mouth. The last conversation we had was a tense builder and the end result was "click" by him. Followed by a text message that read:

Boulevard
[I WON'T CALL YOU AGAIN, GOODBYE!]

FINE, I thought to myself.

Lemme tell y'all that *fine* stabbed me deep. Boulevard's words opened me up even more, only to re-cut the same flesh wounds. I was a woman in heat. And it wasn't 'cause I was horny, either.

I paced the hardwood floor talking to the four walls in a bit of rage 'cause I was pissed. Why, I didn't know, why.

Then I slipped in Jill Scott's CD and listened to Track #6 "I Think It's Better" and I knew that I truly wanted to get to know Boulevard. I started be-bopping to Jill's beat "He Loves Me" not 'cause I felt he did, but 'cause Jill penetrated through to the mean streak in me and loosened me up as my body motioned to Jill's soulfulness and the anger, pain, past woes started to form a scab. I felt an itch around each one and I danced until sweat beads formed on my forehead and Jill's tunes paused, as did I.

Jill's words left me wit' food fo thought and I realized change was good fo my mind, body, and soul. And I began to cry, sing, and dance listening to Jill's woes of life.

"It's not just me."

"It can't be."

"It ain't."

"?"

The days flew by and I hadn't heard from Boulevard

and he hadn't heard from me. It was over between us before it had a chance to start. I made a cup of peppermint herbal tea and sat in the living room and sipped and thought about Boulevard. I thought that I could ignore what I was feeling. *Why do his words bother me so? What is it about him that takes me to another place in time? How come he is able to make me deal wit' the here and now?* I didn't know what kind of a hold Boulevard had on my heart, but apparently it was worth investigating.

11-28 12:50 A.M.

I had gone to work at the salon, but all throughout the day I was distracted by the image of Boulevard. My day was pretty gloomy.

It's you...
Boulevard's words rang in my ears so loudly. *But I wasn't doing nuthin' wrong or was I?*

When I arrived home I ate and tucked my hands behind my head and lay back across the bed and pondered. Me? I stared at the ceiling. Me? At the bamboo sticks dangling on the bedroom wall. Me? I stared at the colorful portrait of me as a black flower. Me? *Okay, okay, I get it! It's me.*

That evening I watched a DVD movie, *GET RICH OR DIE TRYIN'*. I listened to some music. Read a few pages of Sister Souljah book, *The Coldest Winter Ever*, and then I flipped through a coupla pages of Terry McMillan's book, *Disappearing Acts*, and sat the book down and pondered some more. Huh, me?

Out of the blue, I had a craving. Something I hadn't had before. My eyes wandered around the living room. I heard muffled voices outside. I heard a man singing in a cappella while he walked down the street. Couples were laughing. I thought back to Knock-Boots and those badass kids that usedta be cussing up a storm in the apartment next-door to us. My mind drifted back. *I need a vacation,* I thought. And then I felt compelled to do the unthankable.

I swallowed hard. That was my pride I swallowed down. I picked up my home phone and called Boulevard. By the third ring he picked up.

"Hello."

"H-Hi."

"What's good, Ma?"

"I, I, I, was um, just um...."

"Lemme call you right back 'cause I'm driving."

"O-O-kay."

I sat still for a few minutes and then the phone rang.

"Hello." I cut to the chase. "Would you like to stop by? What time do you get off work?"

"1:00-1:30, why? Why, what's up?"

"I would like to see you."

"I'll call you when I get off."

"Okay."

I lay down in bed wit' my cell phone lying next to me. Around 1:55 A.M. the phone rang.

"Hello."

"What's good? Hold on."

Obviously he got another call.

There was silence as my eyes wandered the walls and that feeling crept back in: *Married, Girlfriend, Booty-Caller, Freak, Skank....*

"I'm on my way to your house." He said.

"Okay." I said half asleep.

2:10 A.M.

There was a knock at the door. I rose to answer it. Then I turned the heat up 'cause there was a slight chill in the air. Boulevard stepped in and sat on the sofa.

"Why are you sitting there?" I axed.

"I'm relaxing."

"Well, relax in here." I pointed towards the stairs leading to the bedroom.

"I'm okay. C'mere. Come sit over here."

"Okay."

This is not going as I had planned, I thought. So I took matters into my own hands.

"Stand up." I said wit' confidence.

And he did.

I massaged his back making my way down squeezing his butt and inched down to his *love tool* that was bulging out of its boxers. I moved my warm hands up to his chiseled chest and palmed both sides of his neck wit' wet pecks and moved to his lips, stopped, and looked him in his dreamy eyes, and said wit' confidence and sensuality, "I wanna be in control."

"Go a—" he said in a whisper.

Peck, peck, peck. My lips traveled the sculpture of his body.

"I need your permission to be in control first." I said in a soft-spoken tone.

"I jus' gave it to you, E."

"DON'T EVER CALL ME *E*!" I snapped.

"Calm down, Ma."

"I'm sor-ry. I don't know what…."

I tightened my lips and grabbed him by his hand and walked him into the bedroom. I listened to him get undressed as I lay sprawled across the bed.

"I'm not spending the night." Boulevard said.

I remained quiet. I was in no mood to talk. I didn't care about him not spending the night. I wanted to feed the craving—the sweet tooth.

My lips kissed from his neck to his navel and backup. My moist tongue toyed wit' his earlobe as his hands massaged the back of my head. My body slowly inched its way down inhaling his manly scent as I pecked his inner thighs. And then I maneuvered my way backup and down his hard dick as I glossed it down wit' the hot saliva that consumed my mouth. I felt the moisture clinging to my once dry lips as he massaged my clit.

"Ooooooh. I wanna ride you." I moaned.

Boulevard reached fo a "Magnum" not "Magnum Twister" and coated himself good. I rose to the occasion and allowed my sweet tooth to be satisfied. Boulevard allowed me to have my way. It was hot as hell and the moisture formed on our bodies like we were in a sauna. It was steamy and I was glistening like gloss on some dry chapped lips. I was beaming like the sun.

"I want you on top of me…now." I said softly.

And he obliged.

We traveled with erotic motion to Jamaica, Barbados, Cancun, Italy, Puerto Rico, Florida, Martha's Vineyard, Aruba, and our final destination of cumming—the Motherland Africa. Woo!

I was sugared up!

Boulevard completed his task of pleasuring me wit' his hard rock candy. Damn. I needed some cold ass water after 'cause I was thirsty as hell.

12-2
Boulevard
[10:48:50 AM]
Good morning.
xxxENDxxx

I smiled.

12-4

"Ma, with you I am starting from scratch. I am in the basement working my way up." Boulevard said.

I could hear the frustration and seriousness in his voice. And truthfully, I felt the same as he.

Damn.

He continued wit' his thoughts, "YOU are letting your past destroy you, Embellish. YOU are a very sexy woman. Don't let anyone have YOU thinking you're not. Go in the bathroom and look in the mirror."

My eyes wandered around the room kinda nixing him off.

"I don't need to do that 'cause I know where you are going wit' this." I said. "I got it. I'm still standing."

"Yes, you are. Every day you wake up you should have a smile on your face. It is a precious gift and you should soak in it. Don't let your past stop you. Yo', stop having your guard up because that is what you are doing. All I want to do is keep a smile on your face. I *like* you."

"I like you too." I said wit' the biggest smile on my face.

Mission Accomplished!

12-7
Boulevard
Hey babe...how's it going?
[04:14:28 PM]
xxxENDxxx

I responded by saying, WHAT!
Immediately I got a response back.

Boulevard
Your day.
[04:19:31 PM]
xxxENDxxx

And again I responded by saying, WHAT!

Boulevard
What's wrong with you??
[04:23:06 PM]
xxxENDxxx

I responded,
Right now I am cranky.
SEND.

I responded,
My pussy is in heat.
SEND.

Boulevard
Really…
[04:30:58 PM]
xxxENDxxx

Boulevard
What are you going to do about that?
[04:32:33 PM]
xxxENDxxx

I rolled my eyes and sucked my teeth.

I responded,
What am I gonna do about it? *What the hell he thinks
I'm gonna do about it, huh?*
SEND.

I responded,
WAIT!
SEND.

Boulevard
For what…
[04:33:58 PM]
xxxENDxxx

OH, now he wanna play head games 'n shit! Okay, mister.

I responded,
U.
SEND.

Boulevard
So when do you want to see me…
[04:38:59 PM]
xxxENDxxx

I responded,
U tell me.
SEND.

I responded,
I feel like that's all we share, anyway. U R Very mysterious, which leaves me…???ing.
SEND.

After that last response I hadn't heard from Boulevard fo the rest of the day. I wondered why.

When I arrived home I took a shower. I simmered a hot cup of herbal tea. Around 9:44 p.m. I phoned Boulevard and got his voicemail as I anticipated and waited to leave a message.

"201-123-4567 is not available, beep!"

I responded by saying, "Seems like you're never available." Click.

12-9

I decided to do something romantic or what I thought would be romantic. I text messaged a poem to Boulevard. I got no response back so I went to bed.

12-10

The next day I called Boulevard.

Boulevard answered the phone and immediately started lashing out, "Listen, don't be text messaging me poems 'n shit! I know you tryna be all romantic 'n shit, but that shit does nothin' for me. It all seems phony. You got something to say, just say it! Don't be sending me poems, clichés 'n shit. I don't like that."

"Wait a minute! Why are you upset? What the fuck is wrong wit' you! This can't be 'cause of a text message of poetry. I thought your ass would be flattered! Here I am thanking since you and I is…is…kickin' it that I would show how much you mean to me. And you gonna get mad. You smooth talkin' muthafucker!"

This has to be sexual tension 'cause this shit don't make no sense, I thought.

"I'd rather you talk to me." Boulevard said.

Talk is cheap, I thought to myself.

"WHEN! When da fuck do you make time to fuckin'

talk?!" I yelled.

"Ma!"

I chuckled.

"I can't stand when someone is telling me what I am doing. Who I'm wit'. You're wrong." He said.

What is he talking about, I thought to myself.

"I am not with anyone. I am not lusting after anyone. I am not seeing anyone. Why can't you get this through your head?!" Boulevard spoke abruptly.

"Look, I get tired of hearing that fuckin' voicemail. Your muthafucking ass ain't have no problem calling me right back when we first started talkin'."

He interrupted me.

"*And* the other thing…wassup with you saying that I'm not available."

"Well, you not."

"I have to work!"

"And I take that into consideration. Both of our schedules is hectic, but I make time fo you."

"You know what…have a nice day…." Boulevard said. Then I heard, Click.

And again we get nowhere, I thought.

FUCK IT! WHY BOTHER WIT' THIS SHIT!

I sent Boulevard a text message:

"AS OF TODAY, I AM CELIBATE!"

A few seconds later I heard,

RING, RING, RING.

"Hello."

"Ma, what's up with you? Why are you making shit

crazy?"

"Look, I am having a good day. You the one tense 'n shit. I am not yelling at you. Why the fuck is we always fuckin' arguing over dumb shit?"

"Hold on," he said.

HOLD ON, HOLD ON, HOLD ON, HOLD ON...this is the fuckin' reason why we can't communicate. That muthafuckin' phone of his.

"Hello."

"Yesssssss." I said quite annoyed.

"Damn, it can't be this hard, Ma."

"You make it hard. If you want to see me, just say so. If you want to stop by, just do so. My door is open to you."

"Nah. I don't do that jus' stop by shit. Demand you to cook for me or anything else. I am not using you for nothing!"

"I never said you were using me." I smirked. "I ain't got shit fo you to use me fo. What is you afraid of? Or maybe *you* feel like if you start showing some feelings fo me that I might want more. Sho' I want more, but I know how to pace myself. I've been through...." I cut myself short. *Why bother*, I thought.

"Look, I ain't those niggas. Hold on." He said.

"Okay."

The second seemed like a minute. *You know what,* I thought to myself. *Click.*

About fifteen minutes later the phone rang again.

"Hello."

"Um, I'm coming from getting my haircut. Well, um, if you want I can stop by." Boulevard's voice was much mellower.

"Okay."

I leaped up and headed fo the bathroom to turn on the nozzle to the shower. I had already cleaned up the house. The scented candles were burning about the fake fireplace. The place smelled so good. I walked into the bedroom and pulled out my sexy black panties wit' hot pink cherries on the front. I had a plan set 'cause we both needed to fuckin' relax. All work and no play made us both basket cases.

I took my shower and by the time I had lotion down and slipped up my panties the phone rang.

"Hello."

"Come open the door."

I pushed PLAY on the CD remote and KEM...Kemistry voice was filtering in the air. I opened the door. Boulevard stepped in in his work clothes and looked me over wit' that eat-me-up glossy look in his eyes.

"What time do you have to be to work?" I axed.

"5:30."

It was close to 4:18 p.m.

I felt it was time to step up my game. And Boulevard musta been thanking the same exact thang as he surprised me wit' a strip tease. My eyes spread wide. I slid my wet tongue across my lips. I had a huge smile on my face. *Oh shitttt*, I thought. I leaned back and lusted fo him wit' KEM serenading in the background.

His shirt fell to the floor.

His pants fell to his pretty feet as he pulled them off. Then his thermals fell.

And that was all she wrote as he stood in nudeness wit' his gray hat on his head. Then he slowly and suavely pulled his hat off as his eyes pierced mine. And to put the icing on the cake he wet his lips like LL Cool J. *Oooh*, I thought. I was melting and bit down on the bottom of my lip and eased out, "Shhhhhitttttttttttttttttttt!"

My body shuddered. I was slipping off the sofa 'cause he was melting me down like hot butter. My pussy was creamy. All I wanted to do was eat-him-up.

When Boulevard stood closer to me I reached in fo his *manhood* and drenched him wit' the moisture of my tongue and twirled him into pleasure land as KEM serenaded us along wit' "SAY." And all I could thank about was when he had axed me to *say what was on my mind*. There was my opportunity.

I started by sayin' every muthafucking thang that was on my mind since the last time I saw his fine ass. It was like KEM knew my every thought. I heard Boulevard moan as I sucked him hard and tenderly. I heard him groan and I knew that what I was sayin' wit' my mind and mouth was penetrating through to him (MY BODY IS WORN THE FUCK OUT. I'M LONELY. I'M ANGRY. I'M HURTIN' LIKE A MUTHAFUCKER. And then it got more intense and truthful: I'M CONFUSED. I NEED PROTECTION FROM MYSELF. I'M DEPRESSED. I'M HUNGRY FO SOMETHING NEW. PLEASE DON'T HURT ME, PLEASE? LEAVE ME BEFORE YOU HURT ME. DON'T USE ME? I'M TIRED OF BEING USED AND ABUSED. I'M EMOTIONAL. I'M TROUBLED. I'M UNATTRACTIVE. I'M DIRTY. I'M, I AM DAMAGED. I FEEL MUTILATED. I WANNA CRY ON YOUR SHOULDER, BUT I'M AFRAID YOU MAY WALK OUTTA MY LIFE. I WANNA LOVE YOU, BUT I'M AFRAID YOU WON'T LOVE ME BACK. SOMETIMES I WANNA KEEL OVER AND DIE FO WHAT *HE* DONE TO ME.)

The music put us both at ease as our minds and bodies were synchronized passionately. The heat escaped from us and our lips touched compassionately as KEM sang us to ecstasy.

At that moment something in both of us burst from our souls. Our bodies were soaked in each other's pores. Our troubles had been erased from our minds and we were intuitive of our feelings. My lips pressed against his and the chemistry between us took us away to Paris, so very far away that I felt as if I had stepped outside of my wounded shell. I felt so *sexy*—so fulfilled. I held him so tightly as if to melt him into the marrow of my bones. I tasted him so erotically that I felt a flutter wit'in my flesh and it stimulated down to my French pedicure toes. His soft lips caressed my breasts and teased my nipples so endearingly. And then my succulent chocolate disappeared in the warmth of his mouth. My arms wrapped around his neck as his arms stroked my back and slowly spiraled down to my panties as he meticulously peeled them off of my skin and set them free to fall to my feet. Our bodies were exposing our nudeness as we attentively engaged in KEM's passion allowing our souls to speak in silence. We traveled speechlessly into a zone of complete serenity. This unfamiliar pulsating pleasure engulfed inside of me. Boulevard was in tune wit' me. My wants and needs. I felt heard. I felt appreciated. I felt protected and nurtured. We shared a spiritual moment that moved me beyond comprehension. I felt loveded as a woman should feel loveded. It was magical. Something I could only dream of happening to someone like me. We smothered our saliva upon each other: earlobes, neck, lips, forehead, breasts, navel, and penis, as his finger licked my flesh to feel the wetness ooze outta me. It was more than magical. It was explosive.

I gaped into his brown eyes only fo a brief moment. I inhaled him and felt his heart beating through my skin so rapidly. "Sweet Jesus," I whispered thanking Him fo this magical moment. KEM helped me lose myself in *him* and I was finally showing parts of me. The real me. The sensual being. The loving woman. The nurturer. The softness.

I leaned my head back and opened my mouth wide as tears released from my eyes 'cause I felt so *desired.* My eyes closed as I let him eat me up inside. Eat all of my distresses away. Oh, it felt so good to be handled wit' tlc. I had never, ever, experienced that form of intimacy in my entire life.

At that moment I felt as if "life" was being sucked out of me. Noooooooooooooooooo! Everythang I had experienced in the past was flashbacking before my eyes as Boulevard was holding me in his arms—in his warmth. I felt overwhelmed by it all. It was too much fo me to bear. I felt like I was suffocating inside. Like all of my progress meant nothing. Like I didn't deserve what I was feeling ...*good* fo the first time. Like I was destined to feel misery. Not joy. Not happiness. Not love. I didn't deserve those emotions. I deserved the trauma, the agony, the anguish and it was try'na snatch the little bit of joy away from me. That little bit of comfort. Of peace and quiet. Of smiles. I couldn't breathe. *I don't wanna go backwards,* I thought. I wanted to dig my nails in his back and ax him to save me from my thoughts. Save me from myself.

The pain. *Puuuleeeeeaaaaaaasssssseeeeee, Lord? Please don't take my little bit of joy away?* I was so afraid. I felt like I had just drowned and these massive hands had pulled me out of the shallow waters and revived me. Boulevard was reviving me fo I felt like I was relapsing as if a drug-addict. Feeling like I wasn't 'sposed to like feeling good. All those years I had become immune to bad. And when good entered my life—my body didn't know how to respond to it. It didn't want to accept it. It liked the old way—the old me. But the old *me* was tired as hell. My pussy was tired. Ass was tired. Titties were pleading fo mercy. I was worn the fuck out! But then, there was this trust that led me to believe that I was in the presence of *love, patience and understanding.* Boulevard *resuscitated me* wit' his positive energy. It zoomed through me like an electrical shock. *He* made me feel so valued, as alive as we laid in the still of night.

My warm and moistened lips pecked him from the neck down as we heard the sensual music of our bodies interlocking. Our hearts pounded. Our toes curled. It was the most memorable experience I had ever encountered and I didn't want it to end. I wanted him to stay inside of *pink khocolate* 'cause that was who I was, but it was close to 5:00 and mystery man had to disappear into the night. I could only dream of us meeting up again wit' more hours in the day.

Around 6:44 p.m., I received a call from Boulevard axing if I was all right. I said yes. He told me that he would call me later in the day. Hmmm. I was more than all right. I coulda had a V8. I chuckled.

Fucka V8, I thought.

Shit, I had all of the protein one deprived pussy could stand. I was full as hell.

12-31

I knew that I didn't want to bring in the New Year alone. Every year in Knock-Boots, I sat in my bedroom wit' a bottle of wine at my feet and a wine glass in my hand. I wouldn't normally stay up to wait fo the ball to drop. *What's the point,* I thought. I was in a gloomy mood. So I picked up the phone and called Boulevard. And fo the first time, in a long time I had a pleasurable moment wit' a man who gave me what *I* wanted. He didn't stay until the ball dropped 'cause he said he had to get home to his baby gurl. Truthfully, I didn't know if he meant a *woman* or his *daughter*. Yes, he had a daughter. He talked often of her and it made me smile 'cause he loveded his daughter so much. I could see it in his eyes. I could hear it in his voice. It reminded me of what I yearned from my dad. A man I never knew.

At the stroke of twelve it was 2009, and I felt my life was going to be of joy and full of happiness. Bedell called and wished me a Happy New Year's and I wished her the same. Boulevard text messaged me wit' some kind words fo the New Year. It was something different, something new, and I was truly appreciative of it, of him, of life, of new beginnings.

I could breathe. I could smile. I could cry tears of joy. I could dream. I could fulfill my destiny. Boulevard brought me back to life and discarded my pains into pleasures. God had given me what I had axed fo by allowing Boulevard to reenter my life. How often does that happen? Once...fo me. But it came wit' a hefty price.

2-13

I called Boulevard to ax him some need-to-know questions and to say good-bye. I didn't want to, but I felt that I had no other alternative 'cause he was safeguarding his heart even though he told me to let my guard down. He told me that he only wanted to make me smile. That he didn't know what would come of us. That we were try'na see where this "thang" was going.

Well, obviously it was going in circles. I had already been on that ride and I was ready and willing to get off. Boulevard couldn't listen to his own advice 'cause he didn't want to get hurt, emotionally attached or fall in love. He wasn't try'na open up and I wasn't try'na walk down the familiar street of No-Way-Out so I took a deep breath waiting fo some type of response to all of my questions. Boulevard told me that he wasn't ready to give of his heart. That he didn't want to discuss it. (Funny how thangs happened the day before Valentine's Day, it never failed) I said okay and pressed the "End" button on my phone. I thought it was the end to me finding a life partner, but as fate had it another man was patiently awaiting to venture into my life. His name was London Bleus and he literally took my breath away.

PINK KHOCOLATE

I was hesitant when it came to dealing wit' London 'cause I thought he wouldn't be interested in me. My self-esteem had diminished a bit. Okay, more than a bit. A lot. And during that time I pulled out my Pink BlackBerry hoping it would boost up my confidence. Well, hoping Pink Khocolate would give me that oomph I needed to get back in the game.

About a day later my phone rang.

"Hel-lo. What's your pleasure?"

I could hear the man grunting. It sounded like he was mumbling aloud. "Um, pleasure, you say."

"Yessssss."

"Lord, forgive me for my sins?"

"Excuse me." I said.

"Oh, nothing. How much?"

"It depends on what you want. What is it that you want or desire?"

I heard him breathing deeply like he was contemplating if he should or not.

"Ah, where can we meet?"

"Well, there are a couple of questions I need to ax first."

"Like what?"

"Like, what type of credit card do you have: Visa, American Express, MasterCard or Discover? Can I have the sixteen digits? And what's the expiration date as well as the three digit security number on the back of your card?"

"Oh…it's a Visa. Expiration, lemme see, uh, 11/19. Three digits are 423."

"Okay, I can make reservations fo us at the Black-

Ball Hotel in Hasbrouck Heights. I will place it under Pink Khocolate."

"Pink Khocolate," he repeated.

"Yes, say around ten."

"That would be fine."

"See you then."

After we hung up I felt dirty again. But I needed to do something to keep my mind off of my troubles—off of Boulevard. So I felt I might as well get paid fo it. I started preparing my evening wit' that new client. Over the phone he sounded mature, older. It didn't matter much to me 'cause money came in the same color—green.

Thangs were a lot easier wit' me having my own place. I didn't have to worry about getting my ride from Mr. Rays Garage anymore. I didn't miss sucking his dirty dick. That was the worst of the worst of that deal. I got all dolled up fo that evening. I wanted to Wow this new client off his feet.

After I got dressed in my Kai Milla dress and Christian Louboutin pumps I grabbed my traveling bag and my Fendi bag and headed out the door. On my way to the hotel I felt a bit strange about what I was about to do. And why I was doing it. I mean, thangs had changed dramatically fo me. I had a job. I owned a home. But something was still missing in my life. The pleasures of a man…*any* man. I was on some dumb shit wit' that and God had a sure way of confirming what I already knew.

When I entered the Black-Ball Hotel it was simply exquisite from the revolving doors, to the entrance of the lobby, to the gold chrome elevator doors. Exquisite.

I approached the desk and was greeted by this older gentleman who looked to be in his late fifties. He was handsome. A part of me wanted to flirt wit' him but I was there on business. I resumed back into character. I gave the gentleman my name and he handed me a key for suite 333. I headed up to the floor. And once I arrived at the door I did my usual seconds of mediation and then unlocked it and stepped inside of heaven on earth. Oh, it was gorgeous. The most beautiful suite I had ever been in.

As I was about to get into my working gear I heard the doorknob jiggle. So I rushed into the bathroom to put on my white thong.

Fo some unknown reason I was feeling naughty, but nice that day. I could hear some commotion outside the door. The man was very noisy. And I heard him grunting like he had something caught in his throat. To break the ice I spoke hoping not to startle him.

"Make yourself comfortable." I said, while gettin' undressed.

"Oh, yes, yes I will."

By the time I exited out of the polished bathroom the stout looking man wit' five o'clock shadow was eagerly laying on the bed spread eagle. I took it that he hadn't been laid in years. There was going to be no foreplay wit' him I could easily see that. I felt a tab bit disappointed. I was looking forward to having a little fun before we actually got down to business. It was a whole different experience wit' that man who looked way in his late sixties. Bronze-complexioned wit' small eyes, shaggy hair that needed much grooming, and a face of peace, until he sinisterly grinned like he was up to no good. My chocolate-colored eyes scrolled him from his neck down to his oversized potbelly and I knew he was going to be a handful. I just had that gut instinct. I was a little rusty but he wouldn't have known. "Okay, let's get this party started," I said to myself.

I eased on the bed and immediately thought about my contractual lips. I was compelled to open my legs and have him read my policy stating that I would not be held liable fo any damages, but fo some reason I didn't.

I stared into his dark brown eyes and I nibbled on his hairy ear. *Yuck!* He hadn't used a Q-tip in decades. I ran my fingers across his salt-n-pepper tightly coiled hair as I leaned over him I sniffed. What is that smell? *Vicks?* I continued to explore his body and then this funk hit me when I sniffed his left armpit. It made my eyes burn. *Pew!* He smelled like a skunk had died and was decomposing underneath his skin. He had to smell hisself.

Hurry up, girl. Let's get this over with and get the hell outta here. I took a deep, deep breath. *This is business*, I thought to myself. *You're a business woman*, I thought to myself, again. I could see his mouth moving a mile a minute.

First, I thought that guy was nuts. A little mental case, you know. Or maybe he was on the verge of losing his mind. I stopped and took a harder look jus' to make sho' I wasn't in danger. He massaged my ass wit' his rough hands scratching it up. Then he moved to my lower back scratching that up too. *Okay, this shit is not working*, I thought to myself. I looked into his eyes as I massaged his well-endowed dick and he moaned so loudly like we were already gettin' busy.

"Shhhh. You don't want the neighbors to hear." I said.

His eyes spread wide as he nervously repeated, "Yes, yes, yes."

"Relax. Lemme comfort you." I said.

He vigorously nodded his head so eager to get a piece of pussy.

After stiffening his big dick I climbed on top of him and rode him sensually, at least I tried to believe that was what I was doing. He was a complete turnoff fo me. I sniffed again. What is that dreadful smell? Damn, his feet. They smelled like corn chips and shit all rolled into one. *PEW, PEW, PEW! There is no way that I am sucking his big toe or his dick,* I thought to myself. That man could not stay still. He kept moving his arms, his legs, twitching his body like he was being electrocuted. I saddled him real good and then I heard the weirdest thang escape from his mouth wit' every stroke I delivered he spoke,

"*OUR...FATHER.*"

I humped him harder.

"*WHO ART in HEAVEN.*" He said, trying to fight the feeling.

Harder and harder I humped.

"*HOLLY BE....*" He said, and shook his head like he was having convulsions.

Holly, I thought to myself.

I put my back into it then 'cause it pissed me off that he was thanking about another woman while fucking me. Harder and harder my ass pounded his potbelly. I was try'na pump and hump the shit outta him fo disrespecting me. I got my satisfaction when I saw his eyes bulging fo mercy.

"*...KINGDOM.*" He bellowed, as his arms rose and his hands vigorously shook to surrender to the heavens.

Then I threw my back in again and pumped and humped him as if I was saying "*...didn't I's tells you boyyyyyyyyyyyyeeeeeeeeeee.*" I was pussy pop locking in my head wit' each potent pump. I was pop, pop, popping that coochie strong and then I heard him blurt out, "*C-C-C-COME!*" And then he squirted all of his cum out like water from a fire hose. Then we both heard *vvvvvvvvvvrrrrrrrrrrbbbbbbbbbbbbbb* 'cause he had also farted from cumming so hard. Loose bowels ran out of his ass onto the expensive linen sheets. I scrunched up my nose 'cause his ass stunk like he needed a laxative. The suite smelled like a nursing home. I jumped up and out of that bed while he lay there looking stupid wit' a puddle of pea-green shit underneath his ass. There was no way in hell I was cleaning that shit up. It was the weirdest experience ever fo me. I just knew that I was going to hell 'cause shortly after I discovered that I was fuckin' Reverend Hard-On.

I threw my arms up and ran into the bathroom like a raving lunatic, got on my knees and prayed fo forgiveness. My mouth was moving a mile a minute. God had set me up quite nicely.

Reverend Hard-On talked me out of the bathroom and handed me one thousand dollars fo our twenty minutes of pleasuring. I never told him that I knew him from hearing him preach at Serenity Missionary Baptist Church. I was just there three Sunday's ago. And there I was fuckin' him. It didn't discourage me from taking his cash 'cause I felt I earned it. I got dressed and got the hell outta there.

As I drove home I felt sick inside. I felt dirty—nasty. It was the first time that I actually felt like a low-class *ho*. Yes it was so true. I didn't feel like a "Khocolate Companion." I felt like a hooker. A low-down-dirty-whore.

I parked my car in the driveway, dragged myself out of my ride, and hibernated in the house fo days. It was the worst feeling ever.

About I say a week later I received another call from Reverend Hard-On, and I declined his offer of paying me double to pleasure him. I just couldn't do it. That's when I thought I wanted to throw in the towel fo good. You know retire, but something else occurred that took me by surprise.

A month had gone by and I still was feeling dirty from dealings wit' Reverend Hard-On. But then my Pink BlackBerry rang and I just knew it was the

Reverend. Fo some reason I answered it.

"Hel-lo. What's your pleasure?" I spoke softly, even embellished a moan.

"Ooooooh." a woman's voice sang.

Immediately, my eyes lit up. *I hope she dialed the wrong number*, I thought to myself. I figured I would probe to find out.

"What can I do fo you?"

"Everything," she said in a soft, sexy tone.

I smirked.

"I need to be comforted. My husband left me for another skank. I am willing to pay you cash because that muthafucker took all of my shit: credit cards and cleaned out *our* bank account, and he even took my Viper. The only thing is I need you to come here."

Immediately, I felt empathy fo her. But it was a request that was risky 'cause if I *didn't* get my money there was gonna be a bitch beat down, fo sho'.

"Okay... know that I don't normally get down like this, but I'll make an exception fo' you since your man jetted."

"He isn't my man!" she snapped. Then her voice mellowed, "Thanks. Jot down my address, 666 Clitoris Ave in Lodi. It's an Adult Toy Store, Tongue-A-Licious. Do you have a pen so that I can give you directions?"

"Go ahead. Okay. Let's say around midnight." I said, checking my Movado watch.

"Sure. I close at 11:00 p.m. so that would be perfect."

"I am gonna have to charge you $3000.00 fo my services. That's fo two hours. I don't mean to pry but can you afford that?"

"Yes, and more," she said in this sensual voice that made me shiver. *Dammmmmmnnnnnnnnnn*, my eyes lit up when she said that. At first I figured she was bluffing just to attract my attention. But there was only one way to find out.

I arrived at Tongue-A-Licious at exactly midnight. The lights were dim inside. I exited the car and rang the bell and this sexy ivory-colored woman opened the door. She put me in mind of that slutty chick, the chick wit' the 36DD titties and that round sista's ass. Um, Mandee Capone, 'cept she was brunette. She invited me inside. I looked around at the place...niiiiccccccccceeee.

"Follow me," she said, cutting her green eyes at me. Those damn eyes looked like money. A sweet fragrance lingered in the air as I followed her. I could tell that she was a freak by her skimpy boy shorts that exposed all of her ass. *This is gonna be interesting*, I thought.

She took me in the backroom that looked like a storage room. I just knew we weren't doing nuthin' there. And we didn't. She had another room that was hidden in the back. The room was polished to the "P". I was impressed. This chick had lavish taste. Shit I liked. It was getting more interesting by the minute. She turned around and said, "By the way my name is Pussi."

l cracked a smile, "Pink Khocolate."

After we were on first name basis she dimmed the lights and climbed her fine ass on the center of her bed. Swirling lights twirled above our heads like in a disco of Saturday Night Fever. She stood erect on the bed and did a strip tease fo me. She unfastened her bra and let her titties breathe. She grabbed them, made them kiss, pulled at her coral-pink colored nipples, and licked her Angelina Jolie lips, and inched her finger fo me to c'mere.

I took off my Stuart Weitzman shoes and stood on the bed as we stood face-to-face. We damn neared kissed. Then she undressed me starting wit' my Anne Klein blouse. She unfastened my lace bra and licked my titties like a kitty. Then she inched down to my zipper and eased my Guess skinny jeans down my legs, then my purple thong, and her long tongue parted my already moist lips, as she licked my clit. My head tilted back as my eyelashes fluttered 'cause she knew exactly what she was doing. I stepped out of my jeans and flung them to the floor wit' my feet. She wrapped her silky skin around my neck and tongued me down as if to swallow my tongue. She drove me wild wit' her sex appeal. She was passionate about getting her freak on wit' me. Her slender middle finger eased down my crotch and inserted itself in me so skillfully that I thought I was going to fall back off the bed 'cause it felt so damn good. Then she pulled her finger out and gently eased me down on my back and parted my legs and devoured my pussy so magnificently I thought I had dreamt the shit. I had never felt so loveded before. It was maddening, but pleasuring all in the same. I squint my eyes as she teased my clit by pulling it wit' her teeth. She had me climbing the fucking walls. I started inching away but then she cuddled me by licking my inner walls wit' the tip of her lethal tongue.

I gave her her monies worth by turning her on her back and sucking the shit outta her humongous titties. I licked her lips and pulled her bottom lip as I fingered her pussy. She smelled like a delicate summery breeze and that shit turned me on even more. I stuck that dildo so far up her pussy that her eyes rolled in the back of her head. Then I flipped her on her stomach and stuck the dildo in her ass while fingering her pussy. She loveded that shit. That white bitch wassa diamond. A fuckin' dream. Yeah. She had her shit together. And it made me wonder why her husband left her fo another skank. *What was I missing?* She was everythang any man would want. Beautiful. Sexy. Spontaneous. Successful. A freak behind closed doors. But she was also hurting like a muthafucker and she took her anger out on me. And I was not mad one bit. I loveded that shit! It was the most pleasurable moment in my career as a "Khocolate Companion" and it satisfied me more than any dick could. Pussi damn near turned me out. She was no fuckin' joke. That bitch loveded me down and I was in fuckin' heaven. She caressed me. She nurtured my pussy. She sucked my asshole and teased it wit' her dildo. She handcuffed me to the bed and sucked the shit out of my pussy. I creamed out in her mouth and she scooped it up wit' her tongue and swallowed. The shit was ridiculously sexy as hell. I thought her husband was a fuckin' fool fo leavin' such a freak like Pussi. Shit was off the hook. *But* wit' all the moaning and groaning and sex talk the truth was revealed.

Pussi used to be Prick. Word! She was really a *he* ways back. She never told her husband and he felt betrayed by her. It fucked his head up. Pussi looked like a woman, even betta' than some I've seent. Whoever did her surgery had some skills. She was a sex goddess. FUCK her husband! He didn't know what he was missing 'cause she fucked me reallllllll good. I should've been paying her fo her services.

After our three hours of pleasuring Pussi handed me five thousand dollars. Yes, in cash.

"This is for cumming to my rescue. I am forever grateful." She said, wit' those money green eyes jus' eating me up. Then she tongued me down and escorted me to her luxurious bathroom. The night did not end there. We took a shower together and by the wee hours we were tonguing, fucking, and sucking again. It was the best pussy I had had the pleasure of eating. Pussi fucked me and I fucked Pussi.

When I arrived home I was full. That shit drove me crazy. I had wet dreams about Pussi. I wanted to see her again, but it had come to a screeching halt when I caught a glimpse of *News at Eleven*.

Apparently, her husband had video taped our night of passion wit'out her knowledge. He saw everythang that took place and later the next day he went to *their* residence in upper Saddle River, New Jersey, and shot her execution style.

The next day I grabbed a newspaper and on the front page was the gruesome article. It stated that her jealous husband pinned a note to her hair that read: "THAT'S FOR FUCKING THAT FINE ASS, SWEET PUSSY TASTING BLACK CHICK!" Okay...okay, I embellished jus' a little. It actually read: "THAT'S FOR FUCKING THAT BALDHEADED BLACK LESBIAN BITCH!" Damn, everythang had to be on point.

It hit me hard losing Pussi. I had finally found *pleasure* wit' pussy and jus' that quickly another cherry had been popped.

LONDON BLEUS

Dating was an awkward moment fo me 'cause I was a grown woman who was so usedta being in control on my rendezvous that I never had a real date. So when London axed me out I had no clue as to what a date entailed. For some reason, I added some stank on my blackness. Yeah. I was ghet-to wit' a capital G. I dunno why. Fear could've been the reason.

When we arrived at this restaurant *Eclipse*, London pulled out my chair fo me and I snapped thanking he was gonna feel on my ass. I cut my eyes at him as if to say, *yo' I ain't that easy. Don't matter what I do for a livin'. I get paid fo my clients feelin' on me. I ain't getting paid on this date. So wha' up wit you?*

It was only one way to find out. Ax.

"Look, yo', whachu doin?" I was ready to duke it out.

"Embellish, hasn't a man ever pulled out a chair for you before?"

"Ah, ah, ah…." I was tongue-tied, as my eyes wandered the restaurant feelin' stupid as hell.

We sat down and I slouched in my seat wearing a lovely soft pink Alexander McQueen's corseted dress and sandals. My legs were cocked open showing all of my jewels. There were some hot rolls in a basket wit' butter and a small saucer of olive oil wit' sesame seeds and cool glasses of water. I snatched a roll and broke it wit' my fingers and saturated the bread in the olive oil and shoved it in my mouth. Then I started talking loudly wit' my mouth full as London discreetly looked around at the other couples and kinda covered his face wit' the menu. I didn't know what was wrong wit' him.

"Wassup, Yo'? Why you actin' all bashful?" I axed, spewing bread outta my mouth.

He just smirked and hunched his shoulders. He didn't say what was bothering him so I kept on getting my eat on. But by the end of our meal I was full to the brim. I leaned back in my seat and let out a loud buuuuuuurrrrrrrrrrrpppppppppp.

London's eyes grew big and his face was crimson and his nostrils flared.

"Embellish!"

"Yeah, Yo'."

He just shook his head from side to side and left a ten-dollar bill as a tip.

"Why you leavin' a tip for that bitch?" I asked with attitude.

London was completely caught off guard. His eyes cut sharp at me. "What did you just say?"

I twisted my lips and rotated my neck. "I said why you leavin' a tip for that trifling bitch? Wha' you fuckin' *her* or something?"

That was the last straw and London's patience grew weak wit' me.

London took me by the hand and spoke in the calmest tone he could muster up. "E, you need a makeover."

I gritted my teeth by him calling me *E*, but I didn't snap at him. I couldn't. I jus' couldn't.

"Wha' the fuck you try'na say, yo'?"

He raised his hands in utter frustration, took a deep breath, and grabbed me by the hand and took me outside in front of the restaurant. He paced back and forth as he cut his eyes at me. Then he stopped and stood right in front of me.

"Embellish, I like you. I really, really like you, but

94

babe…"

"What!" I snapped wit' my hand on my hip.

He took another deep breath and looked me dead in my eyes and said wit' all sincerity, "You are straight hood. You say you're not but you are, babe."

I twisted up my lips. "How you figure?"

"Embellish, just because you wear designer clothes. Clothes do not make you a sophisticated woman. Anyone who sees you will say that you're strikingly beautiful but once you open your mouth with that slang and profanity people will shun you. Have you ever heard of etiquette?"

I leaned on one leg wit' my arms crossed and my head tilted to the side. "Nah. What's that?"

"It's when you demonstrate acceptable behavior out in public. Women should always be on their Ps and Qs."

"Why?" I axed.

"Because men like a woman who they can showoff in public. Take around their friends and family. A woman who is not only gorgeous on the outside, but she is intelligent on the inside. A woman they can be seen with and acknowledge as their girlfriend or someday wife."

I lowered my head feeling a bit ashamed. No one had ever confronted me on my behavior 'cause I had never had dinner wit' any of my clients. I had never been on a date before so I was clueless as to how to act.

I swallowed down the spit and looked London in his beautiful eyes and said, "Well, taught me." And he did just that.

London and I did not go out in public until I felt comfortable enough to. I learned how to set the table for dinner with the spoon, fork, and knife. I learned how to dab the corners of my mouth with a napkin and lay it across my lap. I learned how to cross my legs out in public. I learned how to chew with my mouth closed. I learned how to sit up straight. I stopped using cusswords and slang. I was transforming before my eyes and I was happy.

Gradually London molded me into a *lady*. He was delicate with me as if I was an infant. The rough around the edges me had disappeared, not fully but enough to engage in intellectual conversations. I was truly amazed at my progress. I was sophisticated and I even spoke like an educated woman before even stepping foot in a college. I was a product of living proof that nothing stays the same. It was up to me to want something new. All of my life I hungered that life and all I had to do was *ask* someone to *teach* me and London embraced me with open arms.

I was finally coming into my own.

LONDON/EMBELLISH B.

"Embellish B., do you take London Bleus to be your lawfully wedded husband?" Pastor Hines asked.

"I do."

"By the power invested in me, by the state of New York City, I pronounce you...Mr. and Mrs. London Bleus. You may kiss the bride."

It was a glorious November day. Everyone stood, clapped, and cried with joyful tears. London reached in and caressed my oval face that felt soft as silk. He eased in slowly wanting to savor the moment, gluing his lips against mine. My hand touched his white tuxedo. He looked so dapper. Tears ran my mascara as London dabbed my chocolate-colored eyes before the tears had fallen from my chin staining my expensive *white* gown. Then he wiped his moist forehead, as the church was a sauna from having the heat fully blasting. Everyone was fanning themselves with the programs trying to cool themselves off. There were seven fans running throughout the church as we were all sweating like pigs in a blanket. But I didn't care because I was married to a good man. A wonderful man. A caring man. A *white* man. He was a blessing from God. I never thought this day would come for me. With everything I've done in my past. I thought those days would haunt me for life and no one would want to even introduce me as their girlfriend, let alone their wife. If anything, I thought he might introduce me as his *sidekick*, his *piece*, his *bitch*, his *hoe*, you know.

In spite of everything I had done wrong God had been so awesome to me. He didn't judge me for my mistakes. He stood by my side until I got it right. Until *I* got *me* right.

As I looked into London's one blue eye and the other green, they watered so full of happiness. I could feel it as if we were one soul. And for the first time I was happy. London took my hand and we walked as one up the aisle as everyone expressed their excitement and gave their blessings that we have a long lasting marriage. White rice was thrown as we stepped into the stretch limo and headed off to take pictures before going to the reception hall at the Fountain Palace.

In the limo, London and I indulged in flute glasses of champagne and toasted to our future, as husband and wife. We both leaned back in the leather seats and sighed not believing that we actually tied the knot. After six years of dating it was time. But honestly, I didn't think that he would ask me to marry him. There were many reasons, but one in particular was the fact that I never imagined myself married to a *white* man. Dating yes, but married, no. The other reason was his family. I didn't know if they would accept me. That was a big issue for me. But London didn't seem to care about what others thought. He cared about me. Not my body. Not how much sex I gave him. Or, how many times, I performed oral sex on him. Or, how many times, I let him perform oral sex on me. Or, how many times, he sexed me anal. None of that mattered. Well, it mattered, but he cared about me, first and foremost. He cared about what I thought. What I wanted out of life. What I needed from him. He cared about what was on my *mind*. For once I had a man that cared about my mind. It was hard to accept at first because I was so used to men who didn't even care to know what was on my mind. It was so refreshing and I felt so loved.

We had a blast at the reception. Everyone was grooving to the tunes of Barry Manilow, Frank Sinatra, and Elton John. I didn't know what the heck they were doing on the dance floor. To my right, they were jumping up and down like lunatics. To the center, they were dancing some two-step and wildly moving their arms like they were swatting flies. To my left, they were doing the backstroke. I just shook my head off of their no-rhythm asses. Then the love ballad of Clay Aiken streamed through the hot air and London took my hand and escorted me to the center of the dance floor. It was so magical. It was so memorable.

We received so many wonderful gifts that flooded our home. We decided not to go on a honeymoon and just used the money to invest in a home of our own. We only wanted to rent temporarily because eventually we wanted to start a family. So we had a romantic evening in the company of our home. We took a bubble bath together. We made love all night long on the floor. We sipped on champagne and fed each other strawberries. We'd listen to some oldies but goodies. And we talked, kissed, and cuddled. I stared into London's eyes and I felt the need to express myself.

"Baby, I love you. I love you so much." I said, so full of emotion. I lowered my head.

"Embellish, what's wrong?"

"There is so much you need to know about me."

"Talk to me, babe?" His hand lifted up my chin.

I smirked as I looked in his special eyes. I loved him so much that the words hurt scrambling around in my head. *How can I tell him*, I thought to myself. What will he think of me? He may leave me was my final thought so I reneged on sharing that dreadful past.

"Embellish, whatever it is know that I love you." God, his words soaked through my pores.

"I, I…"

"Yes, hon-ey." He caressed my hand feeling it trembling. "Why are you shaking?"

I smiled to ease the tension away. "I'm shaking because I never felt this good before and I don't want this feeling to ever end."

London's lips touched mine and we kissed so compassionately that I felt my heart flutter so full of him. In that moment I could not allow the words to break free. I couldn't take the chance of losing him. For a brief second I thought about Tyler Watson. And I wondered if it was possible for this man that sat before me to be a reincarnation of Tyler. How often does one come across someone with two different color eyes? The only differences between them were the colors of their eyes and the fact that London was white. And yes, the fact that Tyler was a young black boy and London was a man. Oh, I questioned because I had that same good feeling. It was such a good feeling that I never thought I would feel twice in my lifetime.

London massaged my long fingers and looked deeply into my eyes, "Honey, I love you, too."

I swear, at that moment I felt so valued—so complete. I had found my life partner and my life was finally as I had always hoped: Full.

My past was just that and I never planned on revisiting it ever again. I never told London about my past because I thought it would turn him off. I thought he might look at me as damaged or dirty. I didn't want him to feel ashamed of me so I kept my past hidden. I kept it buried inside of me. Pink Khocolate had finally faced her demise and I was elated.

***

"London, come to bed you've been working all night." I felt deprived from my man. I stood in the doorway of the TV lounge in nothing but my chocolate skin. My body was glistening from the shea butter that thinly spread from my neck down to my freshly paprika-colored toenails.

"In a minute, babe, I'm just putting the finishing touches to this canvas. Don't wait up, okay." He said, not breaking his concentration to even look my way. He dipped his paintbrush and smeared color onto the canvas.

Damn. Wha' more do I have to do to get some lovin' around here?

"What are you working on this time?" I asked, while raising my arms as my raisin-colored nipples protruded trying to divert his attention.

"Um...just something that inspired me." He replied, without shifting his eyes in my direction. "Char," he mumbled but not low enough for me not to overhear him.

"Baby, did you say something?"

"No."

"Oh. I thought I heard—" I said feeling disappointed that I couldn't pull him away for a quickie. I was in dire need of some white boy lovin'. My lips were throbbing. My body was craving like a cat in heat. I started to walk towards him in a sexy strut with my breasts bouncing, backside jiggling, hips swaying but he didn't even acknowledge me so I stopped in my tracks, dropped my arms to my sides feeling hopeless. I sighed deeply knowing that I was wasting my damn time so I about-faced to walk out of the room.

"Goodnight." London said, as he listened to my footsteps fade in the dark.

"Blow it up your ass, white boy," I mumbled. "Oh now, you notice me," I mumbled again, while walking into our bedroom. I stood there for what seemed like a split second and then I reached in the nightstand for

Pussi. Old habits were hard to break. And plus, I had promised myself that I would never forget her. Yes, my pleasure partner was named Pussi.

I sat on the bed, propped my pillows, and leaned back, spread my legs, and pleasured myself until the battery ran dead. It was no secret that I had a high sex drive. I was starving for something thick, hard, and yummy to satisfy my taste buds, but London was too busy to read my lips. And I didn't mean the one's on my face, either.

We were newlyweds. Sex should've been top priority. We should've been at it every waking second, minute, and hour oozing sex juice all over the place. That's right christening every room for good luck. But London was preoccupied with work, as usual. And once he started painting there was no pulling him away. His passion was like a drug and he didn't stop until the drug wore off. And I starved like a mutha because of it. So I had no choice but to invest in my little gadget to keep me calm. London never saw me angry because in the beginning of our relationship we were too much in love. And our love kept us screwing till sunset. We had lots of energy, back then. I still have mine, but London needed to invest in some pills or something because I never liked those gadgets. Take it from someone who never had to worry about dick. And now that I was married sex dropped down to number two on our list. Obviously, love was number one 'cause if it wasn't I would've left London a long time ago. The man must've been sniffin' coke to be depriving me. Me! Pink Khocolate. Well, the used to be me.

London finally grew tired and climbed his medium frame within the cool sheets snuggling against my lukewarm supple skin. I was about to snooze into some good sleep since I had fed my appetite. I thought I was full, but once I felt his penis raise my eyes opened wide. I wanted seconds.

A hot sensation zoomed throughout my body and tingled down to my toes. Instantly my nipples hardened. I turned on my side and locked eyes with London hoping that he was in the mood. His soft thin lips greeted my slender neck that lingered scents of honey-vanilla. My right hand stroked his small potbelly massaging it in a circular motion and inched its way down to his shriveled dick that enlarged with each stroke of my smooth, curled fingers that clasped him like a second skin. London moistened his bottom lip. Slowly his eyelids shut. My breathing intensified. My body coveted his juices to saturate me from the neck, navel, and inside of my hungry walls. I eased on my knees like an African wild cat. I bowed my head in the pit of his crotch pleasuring him with my sugary brown lips as I slaver down his penis. Spittle leaked out of the creases of my mouth as I scooped it back up so skillfully with my masterfully hot, moist tongue.

"Oh, hon-e-y," London whispered in a moan as his muscular arms gripped the pillow shams rapt by my performance.

My breast kissed teasing with foreplay arousing London to lick the tips and suction them with strength and compassion like he was sucking the life out of them. Only to resuscitate them back with his prolific tongue of stimulation. He twisted and turned his neck as he licked, pulled, and swallowed them like big gulps of creamy milkshake. His eyes squinted as if he experienced brain freeze and my hands touched his temples and caressed to ease the sensation as I reclined him back onto the pillow shams and climbed on his long, hard, pinkish dick to tempt a night of passionate lovemaking. My lips teased his neck, earlobe, and then moved my body as a fish in water and rode him as we heard the bed squeaking.

Tiny beads of moisture slowly eased down from the nape of my neck, curved and slithered down and leaped off my rock hard nipples and bungee jumped off, and motioned down soaking into the crevasse of my navel and oozed back out as it finally reached its destination to kiss the lips of my pussy. Mmmmmmm. My head tilted back, teeth scraped my luscious lips, as I bit down on them stroking him strong. London moaned and groaned. And that only intensified the motion of my glistening body.

In unison we both moaned as I opened my eyes and gazed into his. My eyes pierced him as the thick, curly lashes batted all of my tension away. London's eyes gazed at me as I liquefied back in my skin. He lent me over and shaded my body with his. He lifted my legs upon his shoulders and sniffed the sweaty but feverish scent of hot pussy. Then he positioned his penis as it opened my wet doors, as my legs massaged his back with the soft heels of my feet rubbing him gently. My body arched as he charismatically soothed my tension into a relaxing state. My head resumed back in its place upon the pillow shams and rested. My love for him multiplied in that moment of serenity. London's generous deliverance of himself satisfied every morsel of my soul. My eyes spread as if to leap out of their home and my lids slowly closed by his rhythmic flow of sensual movements.

Inside my head I heard music as London spoke in words of such soft lyrics that eloquently sung as my insides hugged him tenderly as if it were our last moment of pleasure. Sweat dripped from him and splashed in the pool of my navel nurturing it to drink, to ingest his mineral water. *Ahhhhhhhhhhhh*, escaped from the walls of my mouth as London lips salivated, wrapping his tongue around my tongue like a loop of a string. I was taken to another place and time. Ooh, softly sung as twirling bubbles intertwined our mouth water. The pleasure was wildly escalating as our bodies yearned to be devoured into hours of flesh taunting sex. It was hard. Erotic. Slow. Fast. Calm. I felt valued and soooo loved.

Midnight was stagnant. Quiet was our music. Our bodies made beautiful passion, igniting a fire that blazed with animalistic heat.

I lay on my back opening my sheer legs and invited London to have his way. He gently placed his moist tongue onto my protruding clit and licked it into an uncontrollable state of pleasuring that made me lift my body and pant for mercy. He devoured my soaking wet pussy, ravaging it like a piece of tenderloin. London inched his way down and sucked my toes. Then he slowly kneeled on his pale knees and penetrated me with intense thrusts. His face drenched with sweat as his veins jutted from his temples zealous to burst into extreme delight. I felt the slippery juices glossing my Brazilian wax lips that made a magnetic force cling to my skin. My body smoldered with heat, sweating out the edges of my hair and scrolled down my face onto the sheets. London squeezed my breasts like two stress balls between each stroke, as his back arched, my lips parted allowing him to burglarize my tongue, as we shared the taste of pussy residue. The heat intensified. My back jerked as my buttocks swallowed him whole into the darkness of my hollowness and took him on a pleasure cruise across the Manhattan waters.

London caressed my breasts as strands of wet hair stuck to his forehead. My sexually deprived body ventured him into a zone he had never journeyed. The pink of me came purring out and I motioned my body faster as my ass slapped his thighs. Titties bounced making a flapping sound against my sodden skin. London grabbed the sex-smelled sheets grinding and gritting his teeth. A crease formed on his crimson forehead as his mouth gasped to come up for air. I was giving him "special of the year" giving all I had to pleasure my man. I'd spiral my body around with my plump ass facing him as I jerked my back harder wanting him to feel how much I loved him. To express to him how much I appreciated and needed to be fed instead of starving for his affection. London manhandled me as he flipped me on my stomach. I raised my ass mid-air welcoming him to fuck me anal. He smacked my apple-shaped ass, squeezed it, while steadying his dick inward, inward, inward, until it disappeared into the black tunnel of me.

"Ooooooooooooooooh, ba-bbbby!" I closed my eyes. My forehead wrinkled as my mouth opened, "Baby, baby, baby! Give it to me! Throw it back. Throw it back! Oh, baby, oh, baby...baby!" Our bodies were dripping juices. Lusting sounds burst from me, "Ah...ugh...ah, ugh, oh, bab-y," my eyes squinted. I turned on my back as London's stamina increased us into the missionary position of thrusting hard as I felt his dick throbbing to explode. My legs opened wider strapping about his back like kitty paws. "Oh, oh, oh, I'm," he whispered releasing white cream that stuck to the walls and came out of the mouth of my pussy. He squirted the remainder of come all over my face, titties, and stomach. That shit turned me da fuck on. My eyes fluttered as my body shuddered as I felt another climaxing moment riveting me to fall back and smile. Slowly London fell back plopping his drenched head on my glossy chest. Our heartbeats pumped through our skin as I stroked his wet hair off his forehead. I snuggled my head on the pillow sham full to brim. We lay back in our bare skin for a brief moment catching our breath and then we took a shower, but before we lay our bodies down to rest I felt compelled to share my secret.

"London." I took his hand in mine. He gave me his undivided attention.

"Babe, what's wrong?"

"Um, I have something I need to talk to you about." My conscience was eating away at me. "Um..." I continued to massage his hand. Then I looked him in his eyes and I said, "There is something I need to share with you. It is eating at me but know I am not that person anymore. I have changed, baby."

"What is it?" London spoke in a concerned tone.

"Back when I was a teen up till I met you I was a "lady of the evening." Tears flooded in my eyes and then rolled down my distressed face. "Um, I slept with men for money. There...."

SMACK! London's left hand crashed into my face, hard, and I fell off the bed. He knelt down beside me and placed his forefinger at my quivering lips trying to calm me down.

He started shaking uncontrollably. "I, I, don't know what came over me, babe. I, I, am so very sorry. Please, please forgive me?" His pain-stricken eyes pierced mine. "Honey, you are beautiful and I love you for you, not for who you used to be."

I felt horrible. I fell into his arms and cried my heart out. We lay wrapped in each other's arms and had fallen into a tranquil sleep.

It was 4:30 in the morning when my sleep was broken to get up to go use the bathroom. I gently raised London's arm that was resting underneath my right breast. Slowly I lifted it trying not to wake him as I felt his skin of clamminess. I turned around startled by his pallid face douse in sweat. I tried to wake him. He didn't budge. I called his name. He didn't budge. I shook him recklessly. He didn't budge. He didn't wake up. I panicked and rushed up out of the bed, picked up the phone on the nightstand and frantically pressed 9-1-1.

I heard someone pick up and immediately a hysteric outburst escaped from me.

"I need an ambulance to come to…!" I inhaled one deep breath. Aspirated, "Hurry…please…hurry…my husband. My husband is unconscious!"

"Okay, ma'am, please, calm down. What is your address? Where is your husband?" The woman asked.

"He's in the bed. We are home. Hurry!"

"What is your address?"

"1111 W 53rd. We are on the seventh floor."

"The paramedics are on the way."

I dropped the phone and sat by London's side weeping my eyes out in a state of shock.

"London! Oh, God, please, London! London, please don't leave me?! Not like this, baby." My lips trembled. "London, baby, please?" My quivering hands touched my mouth. *How am I going to explain what—?*

I heard the sirens of the ambulance. I jumped to my feet and grabbed some boxers and quickly dressed London, then myself, in a pair of Hanes sports underwear with matching tank top. I straightened the sheets out, not wanting it to look like we'd just made love. I tried to catch my breath as the buzzer wailed.

I rushed to the door and two white EMT's entered the luxury apartment.

"Ma'am, you called about an emergency?" The brunette haired man asked.

"Yes, my…my husband! He's in the bedroom." I pointed frantically towards the bedroom. "I don't know what—." I stopped talking.

The men hurried into the bedroom finding London lying in bed with sweat covering his face. The brunette haired man with muscular physique asked me some questions while the other man, with curly blonde hair and sea-blue eyes checked London's pulse. Then, the blonde haired man turned and said, "Jake, we have to get him to the hospital, PRONTO!" He had a look of fear in his eyes.

I jumped up and fumbled for my keys off the key hook, grabbed my handbag hanging on the closet doorknob. They lifted London out of bed and place him on a gurney and they rushed out the door.

The brunette haired man pushed the down button for the elevator and then they steered London on. I was all discombobulated and missed the elevator so I scurried down the stairwell, ran out to the lobby, and saw the flashing red lights and siren sounding off from the police car that sat in front. I rushed out the door and into the street as the men put London in the ambulance. My feet were moving quickly on the slippery ice. I entered my Honda Accord coupe and followed them with a face full of streaky tears. *London.* My guilt-laden heart felt heavy in my chest as I drove quietly to the hospital.

When I arrived at the hospital my face was drawn. The look in my eyes told of how I felt inside— frightened. London was my world and without him I wouldn't know what to do. I lowered my head feeling an overabundance of guilt. I shook my head from side to side not believing this had happened. *If only I had let him get some rest this wouldn't have happened*, I thought. I stood in front of the nurses' station and in a calming, sort of crackling voice I said, "Excuse me, ma'am, can you direct me to London Bleus. The paramedics just brought him in."

The black nurse with short hair checked some papers and said, "Oh yes," she raised her full-figured frame from the seat and escorted me to London.

"London," I whispered with tearful eyes. London was hooked up to all kinds of machines. He had an oxygen mask over his pale face. There were little balls of sweat beads upon his forehead and his face was as red as the color itself. I took several deep breaths and then I reached in for his hand that felt damp. I pulled the chair with my free hand and sat beside him as I lowered my head and I prayed so full of emotion. That moment took me back to 1984. The scene was vivid as I saw Tyler Watson face embedded in the red-colored slush. That feeling of emotions burning to escape from my being had also resurfaced but there was no holding back as I came to seeing London, the man I loved with every particle of my heart and soul. I cried for him as I had wished I had cried for Tyler. My tears bled out of me as the blood gushed out of Tyler. I squeezed my eyes tight as if to drain them dry.

"God, please! Please, I have finally found all that I need and want with this blessing of a man." I swallowed the pain back down to my stomach. "God, please, I will do anything You ask of me, please, I beg of You, please don't take my man. Please, pleasssssssssseee, Lord?"

I stared at London in his weakest state and I cried for that man not to leave me. I cried sincerely and profoundly for him not to leave me. I strapped my arms around my stomach and shook, stomped my feet, grabbed the roots of my hair and pulled, pulled, and pulled until I yanked a big chunk of it from its roots as I balled it in my hand with slobber drooling down from my mouth. I pleaded with God. I asked with such humbleness for God to not take the one good blessing He had given me.

"Please, Lord, please don't take London Bleus away from me?"

That November 11th 2015, I stepped outside of my body and I literally died of a broken heart. Thereafter, I suffered a nervous breakdown, which left me incompetent of caring for myself or caring about anyone else.

I could no longer narrate my story. I had become a mute. A recluse. I no longer existed in my own skin. I had died November 11th just as London. Just as Tyler Watson.

All I had left was my inner voice. I had to pull it out of me so that I could continue on with the message.

***

The November climate was damp with drizzle of light rain. The tall tabernacle church in lower Manhattan was flooded with family, friends, and acquaintances. It was a gathering of more than two hundred people. How in the world all of these folks are going to fit in my mid-sized apartment for refreshments, I wondered. Fernando Vargas distracted my thoughts; he was London's partner and best friend. *Oh, he is the spitting image of Fernando from my past,* I thought. Fernando had a huge self-portrait of London looking dapper in his white tuxedo that he took from our wedding. My eyes watered by viewing the portrait.

Everyone said Fernando was the spitting image of Antonio Banderas. He was tall and thin. His long streaks of honey blonde blend with his dark straight tresses that rested against his perfectly chiseled back. His dark bedroom eyes and smooth talking tone hypnotized shallow, gullible, and money-grubbing women. Fernando was a charismatic luring women into his "players" world. He was no different than the women he entertained because he was looking for someone to cater to him: cook, clean, pamper, and love him down wit' foreplay and lots and lots of hot steamy kinky sex.

After about a month of dating those loose women Fernando began to show his true colors. Yep. The male-whore was doing his thang. Sometimes I'd imagine just how good he really was to keep so many women pleasured. He wasn't my cup of tea, but I could only assume that he must've been a animal in between the sheets to keep so many women coming back.

Fernando and London had known each other for years. They met at The Art Students League of New York, and always dreamt of partnering to run their own art gallery. To raise some start-up money they both took side jobs doing some modeling for a magazine called OH BOYs. Sometime after, Fernando stopped modeling to start the art gallery on 135th Street in Harlem called ABstraction.

During the summer a mob of people were attracted to the gallery because of Harlem Week. It was a great business booster for them. Throughout the months more and more tourists started coming to absorb themselves in art. London continued modeling for another year so that he could save up for the wedding. After our third year of dating, I was just finishing up college gaining my bachelors degree in Marketing and started my home base business, an advertising agency called "Bluz, LLC."

***

Fernando placed the portrait on an easel that stood next to the large assortment of flowers. There was a guest book over to the right of the church as people flowed in and sat down. The cherry wood casket sat in the middle section of the room surrounded by more flowers. I sat in the front row in a daze, dressed in a black dress as people greeted me and saturated my ruddy cheeks with kisses. Their facial expressions and many extended condolences made me weep. I dabbed my eyes with the wrinkled tissue in my hand. Then I took a glimpse to my left and I saw London's mother and father who sat lost in their faces. My eyes wandered about the church, until I noticed this unfamiliar woman, French vanilla complexion with bright crimson hair that accentuated her high cheekbones. Her slender frame stood tall like Julia Roberts, with long hair like her too. She wore a large black brim hat, designer black skirt suit and dark Versace shades. The woman hovered over London's casket seemingly in a stupor as if she was pouring her heart and soul out to him. My eyebrows rose, wondering who the unknown woman was. An acquaintance of London's? A customer? An old school chum? I knew I hadn't seen her before.

The woman leaned over and kissed London's forehead like she was kissing a child good night before bed. Then she dabbed his forehead very gently with a white hanky. She stood, adjusted her shades and strolled passed me, not expressing any condolences whatsoever. I turned all the way around as my eyes followed the woman back to her seat way in the back row of the church. I found her behavior quite strange but calmed my nerves reminding myself that I was at a funeral—London's. Then it occurred to me that people react in all sorts of ways at funerals. Pastor Antwone Hines, the tall, mocha-complected eligible bachelor who handles the eulogy beautifully interrupted my thoughts as I turned back around grieving the love of my life.

The overcrowded church stood grief-stricken, mournful faces sobbed uncontrollably, as I nearly fainted missing my beloved husband. Six pallbearers lifted the cherry wood casket and slowly carried it to the black hearse. Everyone led out of the church and got into their cars with their lights beaming directing them through the haze. Tailgating behind the hearse as it slowly drove to lay London to rest at Wyeth & Rice Cemetery, ten miles from our home.

Thereafter, a small gathering was held of mostly family and close friends at my mid-size but quaint apartment across from the West side of Central Park.

At the apartment everyone reminisced about London. I overheard people whispering, "Oh, Embellish and London were the perfect couple. Why did this have to happen to her?" I wondered the same. I noticed London's parents didn't come, nor did the unknown woman. Many people roamed their eyes admiring London's artwork while sipping on wine and nibbling veggie appetizers before the main course. Everyone sat wherever they could find a free space to chat and eat. Some of my white friends watched my Uncle Bo, with his big teeth, thick lips, and jet-black eyes, with rolls of blubber dangling from his dress shirt grab a Styrofoam plate and pile it high with food and wrapped it to go in aluminum-foil like he hadn't eaten in days. *How embarrassing,* I thought. Blue, brown, hazel, and green eyes pierced Uncle Bo and he didn't have a care in the world. I shook my head. Then I smirked as it turned upside down drifting in thought of London. *God, I miss him.*

By 7:30 in the evening, I sat in my desolate apartment at the kitchen table pulling pieces of tender pot-roast and stuffing my mouth. Bedell was washing the dishes and offered to stay and help tidy up the place but I chased her away. A black cloud of guilt hovered overhead as I thought about how *I* was responsible for London's death. If only I had left well enough alone instead of wanting to feed my compulsion for what was between his legs. I needed to be in solitude. I didn't want to use Bedell as a crutch. I had to face my woes like a woman—face-to-face. Although, I anticipated it to be the hardest thing I'd ever have to do. The haunting reminder would remain with me till my dying day. Tears flowed from my eyes and anguish crept in my heart. I wiped my tears with the back of my hand. I shooed momma to go home and relax. Bedell stared at me with a look of concern in her eyes, "Honey, are you gonna be okay?"

I motioned my head up and down.

"Call me if you need me."

I motioned my head up and down again, as she headed for the door and gently shut it.

I gaped at the ceiling thinking about what had occurred between our sheets. Pain-stricken I crossed my arms to hug myself, lowered my head feeling a heavy weight on my shoulders.

As I gazed out of *our* bedroom window, I thought the hours of darkness seemed to come so quickly. The skies had a striking resemblance of a large violet blanket without the twinkles. It discouraged me so I turned away and sat on the edge of the bed in a melancholy state. The skies reminded me of my current state. Everything was dark and dreary in that dwelling *we* used to call *home*. There was no comparison to what used to be. The love had dissipated. The walls, flooring, ceiling to that apartment was just a foundation standing, not a home.

I dropped my face in my palms and breathed deeply. Each room I entered and exited made me feel as if I was decomposing. My world had changed seemingly overnight. The drapes were drawn to block out any source of life. I practically lived as a hermit with only delicate scents of sage and Macintosh apple candles giving sparse light to the bedroom. An oil burner sat on the nightstand, which cascaded home fragrance oil of morning soul. I ran my long, thin fingers through the roots of auburn-brown hair in much despair. I heaved a heavy sigh and then whispered, I miss you, as tears eased from the corners of sleep-deprived eyes. Then my head dropped as my body hardened like a rock and my heart ripped like no-frills 2-ply toilet paper feeling torn beyond reconditioning.

I stared downward at the floral embroidery rug in thought of how much I appreciated London holding on. I thought about how he waited for me to arrive at Sexton University Hospital and Medical Center. *Why didn't I ride in the ambulance? Why did I have to drive my car?* I questioned with myself. London regained consciousness in the ambulance. That's what the EMT told me. Jake, I think that was his name. He said he'd revived London long enough for me to arrive at the hospital. I wiped the tears from my face as I reflected back to that day.

I rushed into the emergency room. A black nurse escorted me to London. His eyelids slowly closed and his parched mouth and chapped peeled lips opened to express his words, C... was all that he released. He gave a motionless stare with moistened eyes. My heart was wary as it raced and I swallowed down big gulps of saliva. My fragile hands were glued to my chest as my blood flushed through my veins. Pulse rose in high degrees. My breathing became erratic. I tried to compose myself, but it was most difficult. London, London. Please, say something? I pleaded as my long lashes batted back the tears. Spiritually I felt him drifting. Hold on, honey. Hold on. I begged in my flustered state. London's eyes fluttered against his flushed face as if he was trying to communicate in code but I couldn't catch on. I couldn't capture his message.

116

I balled a fist, clenching it tightly. Oh, the pain I felt. He tried so desperately to hold on—giving his all. His eyes rolled in the back of his head, thick golden brown lashes blinked uncontrollably like he was having a seizure. He wheezed. I panicked and pushed aside the curtain, hearing my knuckles crack, and then stormed out to grab a doctor from another patient.

My, my, husband. Please! The senile patient stared at me as I stuttered to get my words out. Then my voice rose. Mmmy hussssband, my hussssband, needs help!

Immediately, the nurses and doctors rushed in. I backed up out of the way. I raised my hands to my mouth and gently tapped. Please, Lord, please? My insides wanted to scream but I restrained myself. Every thing was hectic. Everyone was moving around like scattered fire ants, and then within a flash of a second the loudness from a machine that monitored London echoed across the screen—beep, beep, beep, beeeeeeeeeeeeeeeeep, arched lines drawn across the screen until it flat lined. I shook my head in disbelief. Cut my eyes while I mistakenly bit down hard on my bottom lip as my saliva stung the torn skin. No, no, no! I stifled my screams. My left hand covered my vibrating chin. No, no, no! I released as my fingers quivered. I stood still.

London, London. I whispered his name. No response was made from him. It was evident that he'd let go.

I hyperventilated trying to grasp what had occurred, while I cut my eyes over at London. It all seemed surreal. But then reality hit me as tears poured out of my eyes, rushed down my distraught face that displayed my bereavement. Everyone stopped in place. The room was quiet. My eyes widened the size of saucers. The machine was turned off by one of the doctors. Intensely my breathing grew out of control. My chest felt like it was going to combust. I felt woozy and clammy, arms tightened, eyesight blurred. Emotions stirred. It finally hit me like a ton of bricks and I literally snapped and bellowed screams of anguish, Noooo! London, London, NNNOOO! I lost control and started pulling my hair. My body twisted and kicked. I jumped up and down with my hands reaching out for him. Snot was drooling from my nose dripping down my lips, as I stared with bloodshot eyes, veins popping through the skin of my temples. My blood pressure had rose and I felt like I was going to faint. I touched my face. My ears. My head. My neck that felt like its airway was closing. Everyone stood silent. I gagged several times as one of the nurses handed me a cup of water. I sipped as my lashes flickered. I tried to regain myself. Blinking with uncertainty as sprinkles of tears splattered upon my tank top. One by one the nurses and doctors sallied forth through the curtain. I was left in silence—just us two.

I gritted and grinded my teeth face scarlet, and hair disheveled. Finally, I took baby steps closer toward London. My trembled body sat down beside him as I held his head in my arms, as if a newborn. I touched his lukewarm tan face with the back of my quivering hand and wiped the beads of moisture from his forehead. I leaned in and sniffed his hair that smelled of day old shampoo. My full lips shuddered faintly as they brushed against his curly velvet mane. I took another breath, and gently closed his eyes into another place and time—simultaneously mine closed as well. I was in awe. My wounded eyes locked in place. The room remained quiet, as I had no other alternative but to face reality. London was dead at 5:05 a.m. It seemed symbolic to the day we vowed to become husband and wife, November 11th at 5:05 p.m.

Within that moment I transformed into a shattered woman whose mind, body, and soul had died. I stared *endlessly at my deceased husband, twirling one section of his hair, not wanting to accept good-bye, but knowing that I had no control over the inevitable. It was over. London was gone. And I was avowed—a widow.*

The month of December didn't change much for me. Pain resided inside of me as a constant reminder of the man I loved, still love, and lost. That November altered who I used to be. This woman I've become wallows in grief. Where did the spunkiness go? Wit? There was no sound of laughter in my dwelling. In me. No vibrancy. No meaning. No life. My spirit rose up out of me—just as London was parting from me. I built thick walls of gut wrenching pain inside me. *I killed my husband.* I was so mournful that I couldn't strengthen and climb out of all that burdened. A tear rolled down my oval face. I didn't know who I was anymore, other than, Mrs. London Bleus, the widow. The redundancy was a painful reminder, but I had to say it often. *I am a widow! I killed my husband with the power of my potent pussy!* I shouted in my mind as I sat on the bar stool in the kitchen repeating word after word until I tasted vomit at the rear of my tongue.

Then fury sprouted out of me and I grabbed a fork out of the utensil holder and stared down at my crotch with such rage. My eyes were burning hot. I raised my arm with my fingers tightly gripping the fork and I jabbed at my crotch. Then I stood and pulled down my panties and sneered at it. *I hate you!* I jabbed at my delicate flesh with the fork. I was poking and breaking the soft skin as I witnessed it bleeding. I'd grinned feeling empowered by its weakness. I grinned and jabbed. *It's your entire fault, Pussy! If you hadn't been so damn good he would still be alive.* I tugged at the lips of my pussy and yanked at the clit trying to rip it from my body. *You, You, You...killed my man!* The fork jabbed, jabbed, jabbed. *The only good man left for someone like me.* The fork jabbed, jabbed, jabbed. *He was the only man who wanted me for me.* The fork jabbed, jabbed, jabbed. Smack! *You, you, you, had to be so damn potent, Pussy!* I screamed swaying my head from side to side with spit flying out of my mouth. *You had to be so damn...damn...damn sweet.* I sobbed and jabbed and smacked it until I felt the pain. *Pussy...Pussy...you had to be so damn creamy that you poisoned him. He's dead! Pussy, you hear me London's DEAD!* I had a delayed reaction and dropped the fork. I winced. *OW, OW, OW...my pussy hurts* I screamed aloud.

I dashed into the bathroom holding pussy in my hands with it drooling blood and grabbed some Band-Aids before pussy bled to death. It hurt so badly. I needed to get a grip. But it was so difficult. There was nothing left. London was dead. Pussy was at fault. Tears burst from my red eyes and I fell to the bathroom floor still holding pussy in between my thumb and forefinger. I was losing it for real. Pussy and I became immediate enemies. I hated pussy. I hated pussy with a passion.

I tried to hold my breath until my face turned ruby, and then I quickly gasped sucking back in all the air that I could to revive for that second or minute or hour. London, god I wanted to hold him in each breath. To carry his essence in my fullness of bosom that he kissed with his alluring lips. Wishing I could've peeled off my bliss skin and tucked it away in our wedding album for safekeeping—had I known?

I crossed my arms caressing myself in reminiscence of him caressing me into tickles. I slightly smirked. My heart throbbed wanting to feel his touch—just one more time. Overflowed eyes tear. I inhaled missing his smell of naturalness—sandalwood and frankincense off his skin. It was faintly stagnant in that dwelling.

I struggled to lift my spirits up and walked into the living room. On the loveseat lay London's multicolored dashiki. I bought him it last Christmas. I turned my head, not wanting to stare longingly at it. Impulsively I wanted to grab it—to hold it as tightly as I could. To sniff its manly scent of sandalwood and frankincense embedded in the armpits. My left hand touched my neck feeling the soreness swells like a bubble. My eyes cut back at it just lying there. *London.* He loved to wear it when he was painting. Painting was his true passion. As I looked at the walls all of his art mirrored me. *Stop, staring at me*, *London,* I thought. I caressed my arms in an upward motion to calm the shivers in my skin. Paranoid that he was watching me as I had fallen to pieces. Tears filled my eyes again. I compressed my lips trying to refrain from breaking down.

The flood within was overwhelming and I allowed the flood to overflow from me as I caught a tear in the palm of my left hand and smeared it with my right thumb into my dehydrated skin. It dissipated. I wanted to cave in emotionally allowing my heart to grieve. Drop down to my knees and pound my distresses against the hardwood floor. *Why, Why, Why?* I demanded an answer. Oh, it hurt. Damn near choked my being. Pinched nerved me to want to squander in the dark closet and never come out. At times I couldn't breathe freely like I was an asthmatic. And I'd stagger to my feet as if inebriated to touch one of his paintings. It breathed in me, somehow. Through each breath I captured his image in my mind. I touched his passion with softness and forcefully dragged my feet into the kitchen to simmer a cup of herbal tea. It was difficult for me to relax. Sitting with my left leg elevated on the chair as my toes spread staring out of *our* kitchen window wrapping my eyes in the skies—the violet blanket.

The kettle whistled me out of my coma. I stood and turned it off, reached for a mug, dropped in the tea bag and poured the hot water as it saturated letting it brew for a minute or two. I sat back down. A blueprint was etched in my mind. Everything was just as London left it. His chocolate brown Sketchers were on the shoe rack. His teal green bathrobe with his initial L in white lettering hung on its hook on the back of the bathroom door. His razor was on the bathroom sink. Taupe-colored slippers sat beside the left side of the bed. His toiletries were all lined up on the dresser. His olive-green Bob Marley T-shirt hung on the back of the closet door. His faded Old Navy jeans lay on the recliner in the bedroom. His hair tangled in his comb and brush in the bathroom. His Timex watch sat on the nightstand, along side his reading glasses. I hadn't touched a single thing. I couldn't. It was too real. *London died so unexpectedly. It's my fault,* I thought. I slumped over into whimpers feeling helplessly lost.

Captions of the past lured me in. London and I were in sync'. But his parents didn't agree. I was a complete, unexpected surprise when he finally told them about me. Then one day he took me to visit them. His mother was livid due to the fact that he never invited them to our engagement party. I didn't meet them until somewhere in our fifth year of dating. His mother was a piece of work. She was angry not about not being invited to the engagement party but about him marrying someone like me. The bitterness didn't lessen. Mr. and Mrs. Bleus' stumbled with words the first time they met me. They looked at me as if a ghost, a black ghost, had spooked them. I was rather impressed of how well they quickly bounced back into character being polite and all. But deep down my womanly instincts assured me that his parents never saw our connection, especially his mother. She'd always distract the awkwardness by saying in her smug tone, "Honey, be a dear and go get...." like she was shooing London away so that she could intimidate me without him knowing. I held back the burning sensation in my gut and tried to get along. I kept reminding myself, *do it for London. Bear it and grin. Just think you don't have to live with her. Just tolerate her when necessary. After all, she is going to be your future mother-in-law.*

The elderly woman, who stood about four-inch-eleven with silver hair in pin curls, ice-blue eyes, thin lips, a rosy complexion, and midnight blue veins that looked like vines through her skin. Mrs. Iris Bleus was far from sweet. She was belligerent, mannish, uncaring, controlling, and somewhat of a perfectionist in regards to her standards. She had just a pinch of sincerity in her. She was well known for her many years of journalism back in her youthful days. And she was very particular of whom her offspring encountered with. I did not suit her fancy.

Mrs. Bleus' and her husband of forty years had since retired. Her husband was very tall, lanky like his bones would crack if he fell. His beige complexion with liver spots about his neck, arms, hands, heather blue eyes, grayish crown with full beard and mustache with translucent skin. He was a very reserved, quiet, and laid back man who loved to deep-sea fish. London's parents considered his relationship to be from two different sides of the tracks, simply because I was the color of mud in their eyes. His mother never had the chutzpa to say it verbally to my face but the words were written in her ice-cold blue eyes, *"What does he see in someone like you? You're dirty. You stink. You're on welfare.*

123

You have three baby daddies. You're unemployed. Uneducated. You will never amount to much. You look like a monkey. No a gorilla. No a chimpanzee. They're all in the same family. Why don't you stick with your own kind nigger!" My intuition told me that his parents, especially his mother preferred that he dated someone within his race—someone classy ass white.

Ever since that day I never seemed to break through for them to get to know me for me, and after a while I stopped caring and trying. It was too damn draining so I discussed it with London and told him that I was giving up on his parents ever liking me. Let alone accepting me as their daughter-in-law. He understood and believed that one day his parents would come around. But I never saw that day coming. So London loved me and I loved him and that was all that mattered to us.

London and I shared a lot even our birthdays that fell on the same day, November 11th. And that day was also our engagement anniversary. On that day, we cuddled in front of the fireplace, as we nibbled on slices of sweet potato cheesecake seated on the floor, as we sipped white wine. London could never get enough of my infamous cheesecake. It was so obvious that we were meant to be soul mates. Yes. I just assumed that we would die soulfully, one soul with age, wisdom, and peace. I just assumed. It was all planned when we first wed, such bliss we shared. I forced a smirk as I swallowed the old memories down my throat.

I walked into *our* bedroom and sat on the edge of the bed. I turned staring at the last book London read that still laid there resting, *Invisible Man*, by Ralph Ellison, the bookmark still inserted on page 161; he was nearly finished with chapter seven but nowhere near the ending. I sniffled.

I stared in the full-length mirror. *God, I look to have aged within a month.* A pencil sketch of weary captured upon my face. Gray strands were woven into my hair that had fallen like dead weeds from stress. My appetite struggled to eat. I had trimmed down one dress size, knowing that without standing on the scale. The fat in my cheeks had reduced. Eyes sagged with puffy pockets underneath. *I have aged within a month.* My body was numb. I remained seated as not to move the book. My hands shook as I lifted them up and pressed them together as a set of prayer hands. Underneath my eyelids my eyes wandered as I prayed in silence.

Thanksgiving had come and gone as I snuggled within *our* blanket—longing for London. Memories reminded me of him carving our first fried turkey. He eagerly wanted to try out his new gadget—a turkey fryer. London had never heard of a turkey fryer before until I showed it to him in one of the Sunday circulars and he just had to have it. It reminded me of Tyler's mother, Mrs. Watson who had invited me over for one of their Thanksgivings. When London vowed to have it I did not stand in his way. I guess London was trying to please me by breaking his family tradition.

I remembered setting the table that Thanksgiving and filling it with mash potatoes, fresh peas and carrots, cornbread stuffing, rice and gravy, yams, sweet potato pie, lemon cake, and some brewed gourmet hazelnut coffee. We listened to light jazz and absorbed each other's company at the dining room table. I breathed deeply and stared into space.

Christmas was soon to arrive. I had no desire to decorate a dwelling of emptiness. There would be no Christmas tree with festive lights; cinnamon or ginger bread cookies that left a spicy aroma in *our* home. I reminisced. *Behind my back London used to sneak a cookie as I turned to take out a new batch from the oven.* I smirked. The mistletoe still dangled from *our* front door. Since it was just the two of us we exchanged two gifts. It was a token of our undying love that fulfilled us deeply. We wanted for nothing because we cherished all that was spiritually given—*our* love.

It was the following week and Christmas was just two days away. The wintry winds blew white snow as it speckled the windows, and then dissolved. I placed my fingers upon the window and opened my hand and spread my fingers as a Chinese fan leaving my imprints. I nodded and shook my head. *London adored the winter*, I thought. Snowflakes that looked a lot like cotton balls. The trees covered in white confetti. The tourists, bright lights, and noise in the streets—it all inspired him artistically.

The buzzer echoed so I walked into the bathroom and wrapped myself in my white bathrobe and slipped my bare feet in my fluffy white slippers, and answered the intercom. It was the FedEx man with a package addressed to me. I buzzed him in.

It took him about three minutes to get to the seventh floor.

The doorbell rang.

I stood in front of the door and opened it, greeted by this light-skinned gentleman with light-brown eyes. Eyes that pierced mine, making me feel uncomfortable so I hurried to sign for the package and slowly closed the door. I sat on the sofa and began to open the package. As I unfastened the box my heart beat rapidly. As I pulled out the unexpected contents, my eyes began to water. It was a painting of the letter C and on the bottom was written in script Initial. I burst into tears, not certain what it symbolized. It literally ate me up inside. I could only think that it was his way of saying loves you. London couldn't get the word out but I knew what he was trying to say that night. He never said *I* always skipping it to get to the point. I smiled and cried feeling so overwhelmed. London sent me it as a Christmas gift. How sweet. How thoughtful. And attached was a poem. How and when did he make the time shuffled in my mind?

We are one soul.

Love yah,

London

I broke down. I sobbed so full of appreciation for God blessing me with him. London left me with two gifts. I wiped my sorrowful eyes feeling as though I needed to lie down. Tremors took over my body as I stood. I missed him so much as I climbed on the bed and snuggled on *our* spice chambray sheets. I lay on the left side, his side, as if I was holding him. I reached for his pillow sham and inhaled sandalwood and frankincense as tears curved streaming from my eyes. It was too much to bear. I reached for his pillow and held it tight, tighter. Pressed it against my breasts feeling my heart pound and my head throbbed as my eyes squinted.
I'm sorry. I need you, honey. God, I need you.
I cried myself to sleep.

I awoke hearing a car screeching on the icy pavement. I got out of bed and stood by the high-rise window. The snow was about two feet high. I gazed at the ice sickles hanging from the trees in Central Park like crystal ornaments. The sidewalk was hidden. I got dressed, put on my waterproof boots and one of London's goose-down coats, gloves and hat. I took the elevator and walked the streets of Columbus Circle window-shopping.

The streets weren't overcrowded for two in the afternoon. The sun peeked and then hid within the clouds as little flurries came floating down. The flakes dissolved in my burnt orange hat. The coolness chilled my face making my nose postnasal drip. I sniffled and continued to walk as I heard the snow crunching underneath my boots. I felt myself falling into a deep slump of mourning so I hurried and walked back to my dwelling to comfort myself with a hot cup of tea.

I undressed and slipped into my flannel pajamas and reached on the bookshelf for a good book to read as I walked into the TV lounge. I sat in London's favorite chair as my buttocks sunk into his imprint. Many thoughts distracted me as I opened the book and the pages trembled from me shaking. The room was too quiet. There was too much of London in there so I dashed out dropping the book on the floor.

I dragged my feet into the kitchen to make a cup of tea so full of distress. My fingertips massaged my mouth trying to stop it from quivering. Deep down I wanted to scream at the top of my lungs but it wouldn't come out in a scream, more of a whimper. I didn't want to whimper. I wanted to holler my pain out.

The phone rang but I didn't answer it. The voicemail picked up.

I reached for a mug and then sat on the bar stool and placed the mug on the island in deep thought. The radiator hissed. And within minutes the kettle whistled. I stood; reached for a tea bag of Celestial Seasonings honey vanilla chamomile, poured in the hot water, opened the sugar container and added two sugars cube, stirred three times, tapped the spoon on the edge of the mug, and sipped. Then I sat back down. My eyes roamed about the kitchen walls.

On the refrigerator were magnets that affixed pictures of vacations we took: Florida, Bahamas, Europe, North Carolina, Virginia, California, and Pennsylvania. We made plans with Liberty Travel to go to the motherland Africa this Christmas. I sat still with eyes burning one section of the table. The dwelling was a bit chilly so I stood to go back into the TV lounge to pick up the book and go into the living room and sat on the sofa. I tried to distract my mind by reading. I opened the book to chapter one and began to read. The protagonist was bubbly, no, more like ditsy to me. I smirked. Somehow the protagonist's voice invaded me, soothed me with bits of wit as I read to chapter two and then closed the pages as the woman faced tragedy. *So soon,* I thought. I didn't want to know the details of her unexpected anguish. I only cared to hear the laughter as she was in the beginning of chapter one. I nodded, and then exhaled as I heard my stomach growl. I sipped the tea and disregarded its sound of wanting food. Not wanting to move I just remained seated.

I found myself eyeballing one of London's paintings. A homeless man in outer appearance but filled with richness in his heart. London had a way of exposing poverty without raising his voice to conflict. He spoke with colors, rage; red and burnt orange, happiness; yellow and green, sadness; turquoise, pink, brown, and light blue, love; black and white and gray. He said it added richness to the portrait.

Each room had a part of him. Everywhere I turned I could not escape from him. I sulked at the hardwood floor hearing his footsteps walking barefoot. His walk was hard and strong, but the soles of his feet were soft, as was his heart.

6:00 a.m. Sunday, January 1. I wrote in my journal.

It's New Year's Day. Time is brisk. Yesterday, I cried. Just like Iyanla Vanzant wrote. And I never stopped crying. But my mind had wandered into another dimension of why I cried. It was more of a mercy cry. I cried asking God to forsake me. I wanted Him to forget I existed. I felt ashamed for being angry with Him. For despising Him. For blaming Him. I took it all back understanding that He blessed me with six years of bliss. And out of the six, London and I were married for two days. I met London through a mutual friend Manhattan. They were both enrolled in The Art Students League of New York. But Manhattan never pursued her dream of becoming an artist. Somewhere along her journey she fell in love with interior design, and also the man of her dreams Hershel Jennings.

I never thought in a million years that I would have been with such a wonderful, patient, giving, and supportive man. His compassion, wisdom, strength, and persona were genuine. I was instantly drawn to him. His spirit touched me in a way that I never knew existed. It was profound. I was unguarded and I felt safe and secure. It was something about his eyes that were translucent enabling me to see the real person, not an illusion, but the realism of him. I knew that we were meant to be. I loved him when I first felt his breath on my skin. I loved him with an essence of purity. Embodied love completed us as one being.

I'm lost. I don't know where to start—stop. Run—hide. Walk a walk that is suitable for me now that I wear this new outfit. Yes. I call it an "outfit of unwanted skin" that reflects me being a widow. Feeling it, speaking it, writing it, touching it—I am a widow! I want to go ballistic and shout it out of me. I want to stomp making my feet bleed. I want to scratch my wounds about my skin as my body scabs. I want to run in place, adrenaline pumps me to run in place. So I run in place until my heart beats erratically, and I shut down. I fall, fall, fall, to my lowest. I crawl crawl, crawl, to my lowest. I lay, lay, lay, in my own puddle of sweat and I roll in it—back and forth, forth and back— smelling me. The widow. I now have a unique fragrance just like Elizabeth Arden, Christian Dior, DKNY, and so many others. They have sweetness to their fragrance, while mine is doleful. The fragrance reeks from my pores. It stains my pillowcase, my sheets, and my comforter. Everything that I touch I smell its pungency. I want to vomit. Puke my guts out; purge my mournful soul into the toilet as I flush it away. Fully knowing that within the hour, actually the second it will resuscitate itself back into my life. How do I rid myself of this fragrance? It singes my nostrils; makes my eyes tear, and leaves me with migraines that make me toss and turn about my bed—suffering.

This unwanted outfit is not a fit of my choice. I was perfectly fine with the skin that I wore before. It used to fall gracefully. Now, I choose not to wear it if I have to be sized into this outfit. It doesn't connect. It needs to be altered. Preferably, I would rather walk around in the nude and not wear anything that makes me feel so much despair.

Embellish aka the Widow.

The clock read 9:20 a.m. The sky looked gray. Everything seemed frozen in time. My legs nearly buckled as I stood by the window. I hadn't eaten in two or three days. Actually, I lost count. I swore I could smell London as if he was standing behind me with his arms wrapped around my waist. I could feel him strongly—even more when I closed my eyes. I inhaled him. My lips quavered. I was fatigue, feeling like I was cracking like a boiled egg. My brows arched and then fell. Not able to withstand the pain I climbed back in the bed and curled up in a tight ball.

Time elapsed and it was 2:20. I slept for five hours. I sat up and leaned against the headboard as my eyes traveled over to the painting that leaned against the armoire. The painting spoke to me as if London was saying, "Hon-, get out of bed." But I didn't want to. Movement hurt. Breathing hurt. Crying hurt. Living hurt. Death…seemed to be serenity. There were people who have died more than once and described it as peaceful. I could only assume that it would be because everything stops—love, anger, resentment, pain, suffering, laughter, smiling, and crying. It all becomes extinct.

Something wanted to leap up out of me and throw a hell fit. Yes, the hell with everything—eating, sleeping, cleaning, answering the phone, talking, laughing, smiling, and mostly living. The hell with it all! I wanted to hold onto London, every ounce of him because it was all I had. If I let go, I'd be alone—in mind and in spirit.

I plopped both arms to my sides and sighed. I gaped back at the painting. My body shivered. My head shook in disbelief that my beloved husband was gone. Not able to accept my realistic loss. *I miss you.* I didn't know how to start over—to put one foot in front of the other. Gargle. Brush my teeth. Wash my face. Take a shower. Simple things, I didn't know how to do without him. For six years we did everything as one—mind, body, and soul.

Every other day I contemplated if I wanted to wash my body. I wanted to rid of this unique fragrance that stained me but I wondered if it would replenish itself. I assumed so. So I had to make a conscious decision about taking a shower or bath. It was not simple. It was difficult. It took energy to slide the glass door open. Turn the nozzle. Open a 4.25 oz. box of soap. Get undress. Raise one foot at a time to step into the shower. To reach for a washcloth and wash my sore body down as I leaned my head back to drench my hair. It was a conscious decision to make.

The phone rang but I didn't care to answer it. I counted the rings. It was four in all. I got out of bed and pulled open my dresser drawer to reach for a fresh set of pajamas. I stunk. I smelled my own stink. Never had I smelled this badly before. It was a rank, fishy, sour smell. Like, I had vomited all over myself. I made myself take a shower. It was a struggle. But as the warm water greeted my skin I felt my pores crying. My eyes were bone dry, yet, my pores cried like a baby.

The lathered soap was soft and the fragrance was delicate. I sniffed. My hair smelled sour. I reached for the shampoo and massaged my thick hair. My scalp tingled. I let the shampoo sit for a couple of minutes. My body was fully lathered. I took a deep breath, took two steps backwards and let the water drench me. I leaned my head back and let the water rid the soil from my hair. I reached for the conditioner and liberally applied it. Then I rinsed it out. I slid the shower door open and stepped out onto the rug, pulled the towel from its rack and wrapped myself as I headed into the bedroom. I sat on the edge of the bed as not to move the book. I was exhausted and famished.

While seated, I thought of London and me taking showers together. We used to walk around the house in our birthday suits being free from the shields of clothing. Being free, allowing our skin to breathe. His free spirit was contagious. I smiled. My stomach growled loudly, almost like it was having a tantrum. I stood and walked into the kitchen, opened the refrigerator and inhaled an odor that made my nose scrunch up. Quickly I started discarding plastic containers, milk cartons, and the green moldy cheese, rotted tomatoes, and one carton of expired eggs. Then I reached for the butter and another carton of eggs as I checked the expiration date. I opened the cabinet for the black skillet and made some scrambled eggs. I put two slices of wheat toast into the toaster while I brewed a pot of coffee.

The aroma of the ground beans filtered in the air. The toast stood erect in the toaster. I reached for a spatula and lift the scrambled eggs and placed them in the center of the plate decorated with a few pieces of fresh parsley. After college I always had hopes of going to culinary arts school to become a chef. I poured a cup of coffee and sat on the bar stool slowly nibbling as my stomach cramped from not eating. I chewed slowly and took small bites of the toast and sipped the coffee sparingly to moisten and swallowed it all down. Suddenly, I felt sick. My whole body started shaking like my sugar was low. I stopped eating and just sipped on the coffee.

I stood and walked into the living room and thought to check my voicemail messages. Bedell called last week checking to make sure I was okay. She asked if I needed anything not hesitate to call her. Manhattan called to see how I was holding up and if I needed anything to call. I smiled. I didn't bother to listen to the other messages. I deleted them all. As long as momma called I was satisfied because she knew what I was going through.

Bedell had long received a letter in the mail that my father had died. When she got word of the news she was as solid as a rock. And I always wondered how she was able to hold her head up and continue on with life. I thought because he wasn't around it was easier for her to let go. I always wondered if she hid her pain behind closed doors, not wanting me to see her grieve. But to me she didn't seem like she was pretending to be strong. She really seemed at peace and I never understood how she was able to live in peace. How come she was never angry with him because he was not there for her as he had promised? How come she didn't wish him to rot in hell? I never asked her for fear that it might stir something up in her that would make her cry. I never liked seeing her cry.

In my momma's shoes I'd filled. Not having London pitted a deep hole in me and I didn't know exactly how to repair the damage. It was so hard. And my heart hurt so badly. I never thought that something like this would happen to me. London and I talked so often about our future, about having a family, about waiting for that right opportunity to come for him to make his passion a worldly commodity. He dreamt of wanting to shower me with all the things he couldn't while he was struggling as an unknown artist. We both decided that we would see the world first because it inspired him keeping his passion fresh and original. He wanted to have some cushion before we had our first child. It was that important to him and I fully supported him.

London supported me when I first started Bluz. He never discouraged me. A lot of his artwork resided in my office, which was really our walk-in closet. We were partners. Any time he had an art show I made it my business to be there. Just stopped everything because it was that important to him, and he was that important to me. Juggling myself as the fiancée, career woman, friend, lover, companion, was not an overwhelming job to attain. I absolutely loved it! But that unwanted outfit that was affixed to my skin, I simply despised it. It made me feel yucky.

Work. Before London's death I had a workload that preoccupied me. I had to keep the motor burning to provide for the family. That's what our relationship was all about to me. When one was down the other picked up where the other left off and continued the routine until things bounced back to normalcy. There had been many times when I was under the weather and London used to play the role of errand boy because I was too weak to get out of bed. He kept the routine going because we had bills that still had to be paid. The rents were due the first of the month and as much as I tried to get out of bed my body was just so weakened from the flu. Just so I wouldn't lose the accounts London took over by confirming my appointments, rescheduling meetings, and everything mended as if I was doing it myself. We were a team, not only a couple. A team.

I picked up my journal and began to write.

11:11 a.m. Tuesday, February 14th (Valentine's Day).

My eyes are glossy from crying. Huh, this was our favorite day of the year, even more complimentary than our monthly anniversaries. We used go out on the town and have a blast. Get tipsy off of wine, dance to our feet hurt, and laugh so loudly expressing our happiness. God, I miss that. That was the only time we really, really splurged. We'd end our day at work, shower and I'd get all dazzling and he'd get all dashing and we would stand before each other as if we were each others reflection, and smile. Boy, we had such wonderful smiles. And he'd take my hand so gently and kiss my skin. He'd then move forward with his mint breath greeting my face and in the lowest of a voice he could muster up he would say, "Love yah." And I would get all teary-eyed because I would feel his words seep through my pores. Oh, how he'd touch me spiritually.

I would lean in and kiss him passionately as tears would roll streaking my mascara. He'd reach for a tissue and dab my eyes. And I'd break out into laughter feeling so silly for crying but I was so very much in love. Yes, Valentine's Day was our day.

When we would get home we would light candles around the bathtub, and listen to the warm water flow. I'd sprinkle some dried rose petals, and bath bead oil, as London would go into the kitchen to get the ice bucket and a chilled bottle of Merlot with fresh strawberries. And we would kiss and hold each other. He would pickup the remote to the CD player and play Sade and our bodies would melt into the water of serenity. I'd lean back on his chest and he would hold me caressing my wet skin, and nibble on my earlobe as we indulged in intimacy. We never exchanged gifts to each other because we, ourselves, were considered our gifts. Our time, our patience, our affection, our hearts, and our moments of intimacy were priceless.

After we would stand before each other in our purest skin, and take each other in our arms and pleasure ourselves until our bodies were exhausted.

The Widow

Floods of emotion consumed me. I was unable to calm myself down. I couldn't cope with all that had happened in my life. I scratched my scalp. My neck had a kink in it. I was stressed to the max. I sat up in bed contemplating if I should focus on work. I stalled to answer. I sat with my back against the headboard taking glimpses in the mirror. I looked undernourished. My dry skin itched. I scratched underneath my bumpy armpits 'cause I had developed a rash of some sort. My mind was all flustered. And my willpower seemed to have weakened.

The phone rang, but I didn't answer it. I just counted the rings. It was three in all. No message was left only the hanging up of the receiver I heard. I sighed. Helplessly I wanted to get out of bed and feel vivacity again. Feel renewed, but it all seemed like a waste. Why bother? Why care? I had nothing left to care about, for, because everything was wrapped in London. He was my—everything.

Tears broke free as I felt the pain bursting through my skin. I had no control over it. I just let it out when it needed to empty itself. I didn't try to suppress it because the feelings were intense and I was not able to withstand the strength of it. I was not strong enough.

I scraped the crust from the inner corners of my eyes. I ran my fingers through my fullness of hair as strands lay between my fingers, and sat still. I reached over into the nightstand and pulled out a pair of scissors. I sat up and just started cutting wildly. Not caring, but just cutting all the deadness away. And then I burst into tears fearing that I had lost my damn mind. I continued to cut botching my head. Hair was on my shoulders, neck, chest, back, and on my lap, the comforter, and the sheets. I picked up pieces of hair and made a hairball and placed it in the palm of my right hand. I stared at it in disbelief. I stared in the mirror, still in disbelief.

Uncontrollably, I sobbed wishing I hadn't cut my hair. *What have I done? What's wrong with me? London, help me? Sweet Jesus, help me?*

Uneven hair stood disheveled upon my head. My face was plum-colored, eyes swollen; nose was sore and raw from it running. I was left with no choice but to go into the bathroom and find London's old clippers and cut it down to the roots resembling Demi Moore in G. I. Jane, with a buzz cut. I was pain-stricken by what stared at me and I at her. A woman, who had lost her battle to survive the loss of more than her man—her husband, more of her friend, confidant, and a part of her soul. Slowly, I diminished into only a shell of a woman with no substance left in me. I was completely dead inside.

I glided my hands across my scalp only to feel prickles of hair touching my palms. I broke down in an ugly cry, snot running from my nose, eyes beet red with pain and suffering. Oh, the pain. "London, London, honey, I need you!" I cried out. Then I lowered my head. "London, I need you." I whispered. And then I started screaming out loud, "London, I NEED YOU!" For several minutes I did this until I felt I had screamed enough. I scratched my throat a couple of times. I coughed. Then, scratched my throat, again. My throat was sore. I tried to calm down but it was so hard to do. My eyes cut towards the mirror and I just gaped at myself. I looked awful.

Lord, I need help, I mumbled.

I stretched one leg and then the other to get out of bed and brushed off all the shredded hair on my lap onto the embroidery rug. As I stood, my legs felt weak so I stood still for a brief moment and then took baby steps into the bathroom. I slid open the glass door to the shower, turned the nozzle on, and just stepped in with my pajamas still on. The cool water splashed in my face waking me out of my slight daze. I was drenched in wetness as my pajamas weighed me down. Gradually, I peeled them off. I let the water comfort me, as I reached for the shampoo and saturated my hair—massaging vigorously, trying to rid of all the deadness. My arms rose and my hands touched my forehead; they sat still, as the water rinsed my back, buttocks, legs, and heels of my worn soles. I turned around facing the showerhead, as it rinsed my breasts, stomach, vagina, legs, and rinsed between my toes. I huffed feeling lethargic. Then towel dried wrapping me within its softness.

I headed for the kitchen closet and pulled out the Dyson vacuum cleaner and walked into the bedroom. I lifted the comforter and sheets and shook all the hair onto the floor. I plugged in the vacuum and suctioned all of the deadness away. And as I was vacuuming I started to cry. Minutes later I stopped. I turned the vacuum cleaner off and put it back in the closet. I returned to the bedroom and stared at the bare mattress. I balled up the comforter and the sheets and placed them in the hamper. I huffed. Then I walked back into the bedroom to make the bed.

I glanced at the wall-mounted clock that was affixed to the birch red living room wall and it read 4:30 a.m. My adrenaline forced me to work as a slave. I scrubbed the kitchen counter and table until my hands blistered. I swept and mopped the kitchen and bathroom floors until my arms hurt.

During my immaculate cleaning never did I touch any of London's belongings. Every time I had come close in contact I overlooked them. Emotionally I couldn't bring myself to. It was still too real.

I sat in the living room for hours. It was now 8:45 a.m. I heard the buzzer going off, but I didn't move. I inhaled. Breathed in all the smells; Pine Sol, Lysol, Mop n' Glow, Pledge, potpourri that lingered of citrus freshness. All the smells combined made me nauseous. Saliva built in my mouth. I felt like vomiting. I gagged. Swallowed. Gagged. And I swallowed again until the nervousness ceased.

The buzzer had gone off again, but I didn't answer it. I sat still cutting my eyes from side to side hoping whoever it was would leave. I stood to catch a glimpse as I peeked through the mini-blinds. It was Manhattan. She was double-parked. I smiled feeling blessed that my best friend cared enough to come and check up on me. I lowered my head. I didn't want any visitors. I wanted to be a hermit.

I flicked on the TV watching *Lifetime* and blankly stared at the screen until my eyes grew heavy. I put my legs up on the sofa, snuggled against the big throw pillows and leaned my head on its side as my eyes shut in darkness.

I awoke starving. I had never felt starvation like this before. It was not food that I was starving for. I was starving for nourishment of what used to be. I was starving for the love I once had. I was starving for companionship, friendship—moments. Moments were what I was missing the most—moments with London. God, I missed him. It never occurred to me how much I truly loved him until after he was gone. The absence of him was torturing to me. The quietness. The loneliness. The emptiness. The guilt. It was a reminder of my great loss. I had a hole embedded in my soul. And trying to refill it with something new was going to be most difficult for me.

How do I move forward? I had no answers. No starting point—beginning. And then I stopped to think about Bedell. Thinking that when I was ready to talk she would be the first I'd call.

How long does it take to heal? A year, two, or three...? When does the pain lessen? A year, two, or three...? Does the love die? Do the memories fade? What about the image of London dying? Does that dissipate with time? When will it stop replaying in my head? How long does it take? A year, two, or three...? God, talk to me?

It was 12:00 midnight. I sat in pitch darkness in *our* bedroom. My mind was playing tricks on me. This "inner voice" was influencing me to sit in darkness and just wait. What I am waiting for, I wondered. The "inner voice" whispered London.

It was April 1st and the April fool was me. This "inner voice" told me to wait because London was coming. It said that I should sit still and be patient. Believe...that his spirit was coming to deliver a message to me. It was almost six months and he hadn't come to me in my dreams. But I felt his aura around me. I wanted to see him standing before me one last time. To see with my very own eyes that he was no longer suffering. I'd hoped that he was at peace. Tears ran from my eyes. I remained still believing that he was coming. It was 3:00 a.m. and London hadn't come. I felt like he had abandoned me. Baby, come to me, please? I mumbled in desperation.

It was 6:00 a.m. and London hadn't come. I stopped yearning and just imagined him in my thoughts.

***

The days were becoming days of simplicity for me. I was able to get out of bed freely, take a shower or bath on a daily basis. I was climbing out of my well of grief. I hung London's picture, C in the living room about our fireplace. I opened the drapes inviting the sun light into *our* home. I talked often to God to relay messages to London for me. Sometimes I spoke of him in the present tense. I felt as though he was going to one-day walk through the door and embrace me with a hug and kiss. It was still too early for me to remove his belongings. Every room I looked in he was there. I was not going to move out and distance myself from him. Trying to run from my past/present/future pains wouldn't solve a thing. London was a part of me. And as much as I mourned for him I felt myself evolving. The hurt was not as stinging. It was a tug-a-war because I would go up and down in emotions but I was optimistic that I would overcome the pains. I took small steps to recover. I needed to grieve and at times it hit me like a bolt of lightening. At times I felt I couldn't go on without him. And when those times came about I simply prayed. That was my regimen: prayer. I prayed for peace on earth as it is in heaven.

I indulged in work. I picked up a couple of accounts and had been preoccupying my mind with trying to be creative in my thoughts. Things were slowly coming to amend. I was starting to feel like myself. Look like me, again. I still hadn't spoken to Bedell. Manhattan had been reaching out but I hadn't returned any of her calls, either. Actually, I hadn't returned any calls. I wasn't ready to hear the empathy condolences. Even after so many months people still didn't know how to address an issue such as death. They would get tongue-tied. Not wanting to say the wrong thing to upset the person. I was trying to regain, rebuild, to strengthen what was left of me. Time. *I just need more time,* I thought to myself.

I hadn't been outdoors, other than when I took that walk, took out the trash, checked the mailbox, and sat on the balcony for some fresh air. I kept away from people trying to accept London's absence. It was hard. The drastic changes I had to undergo were unbearable. But I was coping the best I could.

The June air smelled sweet. Flowers bloomed round the trees. I stepped out onto the balcony and sat down reminiscing about all the times London and I had sat out on the balcony together, cuddled, kissed, and hugged. I imagined our early years as a couple. We shared something very special.

The light air brushed against my face. I had a slight glow. I exhaled, still in disbelief, but believing that London was gone, but feeling like he was so very much alive in my heart. As I was reminiscing in thought of him I heard the phone rang so I leaped up and dashed in to answer it.

"Hello."

"Well, it's about damn time. Are you okay, Embellish? I've been calling, calling and calling. Coming by. And you haven't even bothered to return my calls."

"Yes, Manhattan, I am doing well. Sorry about not returning your calls but it hasn't been easy for me." I lowered my head, not wanting sorrow to smother me.

"I understand. Say no more." Manhattan sighed. "When was the last time you've been out of the house?"

"I was just out on the balcony."

"No, no, I mean, out?"

"I haven't."

"I'm on my way." Manhattan said, quickly hanging up the phone.

"No...." I said, in a delayed response.

I'm not ready to be around anyone. I'm not ready to re-enter the world.

I huffed.

Within a half hour Manhattan was buzzing. I walked slowly to the intercom to let her in, breathed, and then opened the door once she knocked. As soon as I opened the door Manhattan's eyes scrolled me precisely, every detail of me.

"Come in." I said, offering Manhattan a drink, which she accepted.

We walked into the kitchen and I opened the

refrigerator and poured us two tall glasses of freshly made lemonade. And then we stepped out onto the balcony to chat amongst the noisy, busy streets.

"Tell me, are you really holding up?" Manhattan asked, as she stared piercingly into my eyes.

I shrugged my shoulders. Not wanting to share too much, too soon.

"How are you?" I asked, trying to divert the focus off of me.

"I'm fine. Nothings really changed since we've last spoken. I'm free. The divorce was finalized sometime after London's …well, you know."

"Oh, I'm sorry." I said with sincerity.

"No, no, don't be. Hershel and I just disconnected." She smiled. "He was a good black man all and all. I think we grew apart. His wants, needs, were no longer what I wanted and needed. I have no regrets. We gave it *our* best shot."

I smirked feeling a bit uncomfortable. I tried to listen as Manhattan released her burdens.

"Enough of me dwelling, what's been going on with you? Have you gone back to work, yet?" she asked.

"Actually…yes. It's hard getting back into the swing of things."

"I bet."

"Um, have you started packing L…..?" Manhattan caught herself.

Suddenly, I burst into tears. Manhattan stood and knelt down to comfort me.

"I'm sorry." Manhattan slapped herself on the forehead. "Honey, I'm so sorry to have upset you."

"No, no, it's okay. This is a part of the healing process, right?"

Manhattan nodded her head. We both cracked a smile.

"Would you like to stay for brunch?" I asked.

"Sure, as long as I can help."

We hugged, and then stepped back inside for me to prepare us a delicate and delicious meal of crab cakes with cranberry and apples and spinach salad with a splash of balsamic vinegar. The day turned out to be pretty wonderful. How lucky was I to have such an awesome best friend. Very.

The October rain broke my sleep. I rose from my bed that Saturday, took a shower, got dressed, and headed out to the supermarket. It felt weird being around people. As I was heading in the produce section my cell phone rang.

"Hello."

"Hi. You're up and about awfully early."

"Yes, Manhattan, I needed to pick up some groceries. I like to get here before the herd of people comes. I hate when people pick over things."

"I'm the same way." Manhattan laughed. "Well, the reason I called is because I have two tickets to see "Bridge and Tunnel" would you like to go?"

"What's Bridge and Tunnel?"

"Oh, it's a one-woman show with Sarah Jones. She is performing at the Helen Hayes Theater here in the city."

"Oh. Have you heard the reviews of the show?"

"There you go, Embellish. The analytical beast is reborn. Honey, try to be a little spontaneous."

"You're right." I said.

"The show starts around seven. I'll call you when I'm on my way."

"Okay. Good-bye."

As I ended the call I caught a man staring in my direction. Was I talking too loudly, I wondered? I continued reviewing my shopping list and filled my cart and then I got in line at the checkout counter. The same man from the produce section walked passed me and continued to stare, almost like he was flirting with his eyes. I smirk feeling a bit flattered. I paid the cashier and headed to my car. I packed my trunk, got in the car, and drove off.

On my way home I stopped at Wal-Mart to pick up some items. As I walked through the aisle I stopped in the music section. I picked up two CDs "Back to Bedlam" by James Blunt and Corinne Bailey Rae. I grabbed three DVDs, *The Lake House, Something New,* and *Why Did I Get Married* and picked up some Tide Downy. Then I headed towards the checkout line. Being out and about was a start to my recovery. As I stood in line I witnessed couples, families together, and it made me a little sad because I felt myself springing back into my grieving stages. Anything seemed to trigger it and the only things that I could do was accept it, acknowledge it, and pray to keep moving forward with my life. A life that felt empty, almost like half a life, but still in all a life and I had to come to grips with empowering myself. No one could help me with the internal wounds that mutilated my flesh. Only I could soothe me with the ointment of patience. And as much as I would have liked a speedy recovery I knew that it was not in my best interest to rush things because I wouldn't fully heal. If anything, I would sink back into a world of reclusion.

After shopping, I returned home to settle in. I was exhausted. I put away the groceries and made a sandwich and watched a little TV. Around five o'clock I lay out a pair of trousers and a turtle neck sweater and a pair of Michael Kors boots to go with Manhattan to see the one-woman show.

The phone rang.

"Hello."

"Hi. How are you doing, sweetie? I've been trying to reach you but I figured you had reasons for not answering your phone so I gave you time to be to yourself."

"Thanks, Momma." I smiled. "I'm fine. Everyday is a new day. New feelings. A new wound to heal, you know?"

"Yes, Lord, sweetie, you just take your time. It's difficult at first, but with time the wounds begin to heal, and sometimes they re-open, and heal. It's so unpredictable. You'll be fine."

"Momma, I really needed to hear that."

"Well, I'm not going to take up much of your time. Call if you need me, even to talk, okay."

"Yes."

After I hung up with momma I felt a sense of contentment within. Each day was a day to kind of rejoice because I was coming along. The pain was still real, torturing at times, but I managed to cope. If things got too distressing I'd cry, if needed just for an outlet.

I took a shower and got dressed.

Twenty minutes later, the buzzer wailed in its annoying tone so I rose to my feet, grabbed my things, and headed for the door. As I was stepping off the elevator I saw Manhattan lent down wiping off her Baby-Phat stiletto boots with a napkin. She accentuated her look with some black leather pants and a camel wool sweater with her three-quarter-length leather jacket on. Her dreadlocks were twisted in a flattering style that enhanced her natural beauty. As I was walking towards her she looked up and subtly looked me over with her bold hazel eyes that brought out her chestnut-brown complexion. Then she smiled.

"You look great, Embellish!"

I took in her compliment and said, "Thanks, so do

you."

Manhattan led the way to her red Mercedes and we jumped in, buckled up, and headed off.

After the show, Manhattan and I went to a Portuguese restaurant. The restaurant was packed to capacity. The music was subtle and soft. We sat and just absorbed the atmosphere, minutes into our conversation Manhattan excused herself to go to the ladies room. As I sat there this attractive black woman who was seated across from me with two other guests tapped me on my shoulder. I turned to look in her direction.

"Yes." I said.

"I love your haircut, Miss! I was never bold enough to cut my hair, and plus, every barber shop I attempted my mother beat me to the punch by threatening the barber." She laughed.

"Thank you." I said, with a cracked smile.

The woman resumed back to her guests and I took a couple sips of water. Manhattan returned and was smiling from ear to ear.

"Embellish, I took the liberty of ordering us lobster. Is that okay with you?"

"Sure."

I felt a bit uncomfortable being around so many people but I found myself easing out of my uncomfortable zone and relaxing.

The waiter served us hot bread while we waited for our main course. We nibbled on salad to nourish our taste buds.

About twenty minutes later the waiter came with two big platters of lobster with bake potatoes, mixed vegetables, and a side of sour cream and melted butter. We placed our bibs on, laid our napkins on our laps, and enjoyed our meals as we sipped on white wine and chatted till our hearts were content.

When I arrived home I plopped on the sofa. I was full to the brim. I checked my messages hearing Fernando's voice.

"Hi, Embellish. Listen, I hate to call you with business but I need to know what you plan on doing as far as this partnership. I would love to keep the gallery open but I need to either buy you out or maybe you would want to consider being my partner. Please call me as soon as possible?"

I picked up the phone and called him.

"ABstractions, Fernando speaking."

"Hi, Fernando, it's Embellish. Listen, it never dawned on me as to what I would do if this happened. The business was London's life. I can't just disregard that so I feel we should remain partners. I'll call our lawyer Monday to see how to go about handling this. Other than that, how are you doing?"

"Oh fine, sweetie, just fine. I'm trying to attract some traffic up in here. We have a lot more tourists who seem to admire London's work, especially this one woman, every weekend she comes admiring that piece called, "A Mother's Womb.""

"Oh really! That's a gorgeous piece. It's like six grand... right?"

"Yes, hon-ey. I wish she would stop eyeballing it and buy the damn thing. Hell, she can ogle at it as much as she wants in the company of her own home." Fernando laughed.

"Have you sold any of his art pieces?"

"Actually, some tourists asked about certain pieces but no one has bid as of yet. What I want to do with your permission of course, is use the black and white photo that I took of him when we were modeling and write a piece on him in remembrance of his love for art. Not many know of him but once they know that he is no longer with us I think it will create a buzz."

"Listen, whatever will help keep the business flowing I am all for it."

"Thanks Embellish."

"No. Thank you."

After we hung up I walked into *my* bedroom and searched in the nightstand drawers for the lawyer, Mr. RJ Needle's business card. I lay it on top of the dresser to remind myself to call him come Monday.

Around 10:40 a.m. I awoke rejuvenated. I sat up and gaped at the ceiling and said, "Good morning," to God and London. Then I slipped out of bed and walked into the bathroom to freshen up. Afterwards, I headed towards the kitchen to brew a pot of coffee. I snapped my fingers remembering to call Mr. Needle about changing over the partnership from London to me. I walked back into the bedroom and grabbed the business card on the edge of the dresser and picked up the phone to call.

"Mr. RJ Needle's office, how may I help you?" A woman spoke in a pleasant tone.

"Good morning, may I speak with Mr. Needle, please?"

"Who may I ask is calling?"

"Mrs. Bleus."

"Hold, please?"

I waited a few seconds.

"Mr. Needle speaking," he spoke in a deep voice.

"Good morning, this is Mrs. Bleus."

"What a delight. Oh, I'm sorry about your loss. I'm sorry I couldn't make the funeral I was out of town. Such a shock. Well, how are you doing, Mrs. Bleus?"

"Well, I'm doing fine. I'm calling about my husband's partnership with Mr. Fernando Vargas of the art gallery ABstractions. I wanted to know how I would go about changing the name over to me. Um, I don't want Fernando to buy me out I would rather keep the business in remembrance of London since he loved it so much."

"I see. Well, it's not a complicated process. I would just need to see you and Mr. Vargas to sign some papers."

"Oh, okay. So…what day is good for you?" I asked.

"I'm free tomorrow around 2:00."

"Okay. Two o'clock it is."

"Good-bye."

"Good-bye, Mrs. Bleus."

I immediately called Fernando to give him the details and we decided for him to pick me up tomorrow and drive to Mr. Needle's here in New York.

The rest of the day I just moped around the house bored out of my mind.

I got up about 9:00 a.m. on Tuesday. I made some grits and hickory smoke-bacon. Toasted some potato bread and simmered some hot water for a cup of tea. I drifted into space reliving the grand opening of ABstractions. Then I smiled. London was so thrilled. I could see it in his eyes—those special eyes. It was his dream comes true. I stood to turn the bacon and stir the grits. After I ate and tidied up the place, (leaving all London's belongings intact). It still was too difficult to move them because I believed I would be burying his memory. He was too much a part of me. I left everything, as it was to keep him alive. It was the only way I could cope at that present time. I needed to sense him around me. I needed to see things that he used. I just needed him.

I slipped one of Anthony Hamilton's CDs in the CD player giving myself a moment to relax before Fernando arrived. I thought I would relax until I heard him singing, "Pass Me Over" and tears engulfed in my eyes. I wasn't sad. I felt myself growing, and if I should die for whatever reason, at least my life had journeyed in another direction. I had been to hell and back but I wasn't giving in or up. For once, I was proud of myself. At 1:15 p.m. Fernando buzzed and I pushed the intercom button letting him know that I was on my way downstairs.

We met with Mr. Needle promptly at 2:00. His secretary, Nancy asked us to have a seat while she let him know of our arrival. Nancy sat with her short brunette bob and freckled nose with the prettiest skin that looked like she had a permanent blush. Her eyes were the size of almonds with dots of blue crystal. She was medium build with discolored yellowish teeth and a friendly disposition.

The office was relatively quiet except for the ringing of the phone. Nancy seemed bombarded with calls and her hands couldn't seem to move as quickly as her mouth spoke. Fernando and I chitchatted and he gave me the heads up on what's happening at the gallery since we spoke yesterday.

"Embellish, I did the write-up on London and I was wondering if you wouldn't mind taking a look at it. Give me some feedback before it goes to print?"

"Sure."

Five minutes into our conversation Mr. Needle stepped out of his office and greeted us with a smile. He stood in his navy-blue suit with his rotund stomach bulging out of his light blue dress shirt. His receding hairline and clean-shaven face was well groomed. His dark brown shoes shined to perfection.

"Come...please, come in." Mr. Needle said in a enthused tone.

Fernando and I both stood and shook Mr. Needles hand and walked into his office. I couldn't remember the last time I was there. It might have been when I started my business.

"Please, have a seat you two. Would you like

anything to drink…coffee, tea, or water?"

Fernando and I spoke in unison, "No thanks."

"Very well…let's get down to business shall we. Mrs. Bleus you stated you wanted to change over the name from your husband's to yours."

"Yes."

Fernando interjected, "Mr. Needle, here are the copies of my original paperwork that London and I signed."

He handed them to Mr. Needle.

Mr. Needle opened his desk drawer frantically searching for a file. His eyes widened. "Ah…here we go, Mrs. and Mrs. Bleus."

He opened the folder and opened Fernando's to compare. He had a puzzling look upon his face.

"Mr. Needle is there something wrong?" I asked.

"Well, Mrs. Bleus, I don't seem to have the paperwork for ABstractions. I only have the paperwork for the advertising agency."

"How can that be? London and I came together to see you."

"Yes. I remember. Oh how embarrassing." Mr. Needle scratched his scalp and then hit the speaker button on his phone and called Nancy into his office.

"Yes, sir," she said.

A few minutes later, Nancy walked in Mr. Needle's office with a pen and pad in hand.

"Nancy, the Bleus' folder seems to be missing some forms from Mr. Bleus' business. Do you know, why?"

Nancy stood pondering. "Oh…oh, yes. I remember. One moment, please?"

Nancy walked out of the office and then returned with an appointment book in her hands. She laid it on his desk backtracking until she saw London's name.

Nancy pointed her index finger on the page. "Yes here, it was in August.…"

I stood to look at what she was talking about.

"Mr. Bleus came in with his mother and asked for his original forms. I remember overhearing his mother say something about a new lawyer. What was his name...ah...Vista. I jotted down the name to inform you, Mr. Needle of the change. I guess I forgot to tell you. Oh, dear. Well, his name is Andrew Vista."

"That doesn't make any sense. London and I always discussed our business affairs. We didn't have any secrets. He never mentioned anything about coming here with his mother or hiring another lawyer."

Fernando sat with a perplexed look on his face.

I massaged my temples.

"What's going on?" I said aloud.

Fernando stood to pat me on my back.

Mr. Needle extended his hand and offered an apology.

"Thanks, Mr. Needle and Nancy for your time." I said with a flustered look on my face.

Fernando and I both shook Mr. Needle's hand and walked out of his office. Fernando and I headed back to my apartment to sort things out.

In his car there was complete silence. Not even the radio was playing. Both of us seemed flustered. *Why would London keep this from me?* I rubbed my eyes because I had gained a headache.

When we arrived back at my home Fernando sat down on the sofa as I rummaged through all of my important paperwork in the bedroom. Nothing. There was nothing with an Andrew Vista on it. I exhaled quite disgusted. Fernando yelled out from the living room,

"Embellish, I'm going to go to the gallery to see if maybe there is something there."

"Okay. Call me."

My hands covered my troubled face as I sat on the edge of the bed still not moving the book in a complete fog.

About an hour later, Fernando called me and told me that he found Andrew Vista's business card in London's desk. As we were talking Fernando asked me to hold that thought. He put me on mute.

Then he returned, "Honey, I'm gonna have to call you back I have a customer."

"All right."

We hung up.

I sat with my feet up on the sofa and my arms resting on my knees thinking. I glared at each portrait of London's brewing inside. I found myself talking to the portraits as if they were going to talk back. My headache turned into a migraine. About a half hour later, Fernando called me back. He sounded full of excitement.

"Embellish, you are not going to believe what just happened a few minutes ago!"

"What?"

"One of London's paintings was just bought."

"Which one?"

"A Mother's Womb!"

"What!"

"Yes…yes, this woman. As a matter-of-fact, the same woman who has been ogling it for the past couple of weekends came strolling in here and paid cash for it."

"She paid six thousand dollars in cash?!"

"Yes siree."

"What does she look like? I mean, does she look like she has that kind of money?"

"Well, she was tall like a model, flawless ivory skin with cherry red lipstick lips, and high cheekbones like Bo Derek. Her hair was bright red and long like Julia Roberts. Ms. Money was dress to kill. I'd bang her."

"What!"

Fernando cut to the chase. "The woman is drop-dead gorgeous. Well, I just had to share that with you. This is a start in the right direction. I am going to pull out some of his old paintings from our stockroom and see who bites."

"Sounds good...sounds...."

"Honey, are you okay?"

"I'm just trying to figure things out. Not trying to rain on your parade. I'm happy that things are going well at the gallery. London would be proud."

"Yes, he would. Okay, love, I'll call you later."

After we hung up I sat in the same spot for what seemed like hours. *Red hair...Julia Roberts. Why does that sound like the woman who was at London's funeral? Who is this woman? And how does she know London?* I was an emotional wreck and I couldn't seem to get it together.

The phone rang.

"Hello."

"Hi, honey."

"Hi, Momma."

"What's wrong, Embellish? You sound down."

"Oh, momma, what's right? Today, Fernando and I went to Mr. Needle's office to change over London's name to mine for the gallery. Well, come to find out London and his mom had gone years prior and London hired another lawyer without consulting me. Ma, he never told me."

"What! That doesn't sound like the London we knew."

"I know. I can only think the worse and that being his mother put him up to it."

"Honey, you can't jump to conclusions."

"I know. But...."

"You're gonna have to dig a little deeper, possibly speak to the new lawyer if you can find him."

"Yeah, then today at the gallery Fernando called me and said a woman came in and bought London's "A Mother's Womb," painting for six thousand dollars in cash."

"Cash!" Bedell shrieked.

"Yes, cash, Ma. I was thrilled but it sounded a little strange."

"People are people, honey, not everyone does things the same. She might have been one of those wealthy women who don't like to write out checks."

"Yeah, who don't like to use credit cards either?" I chuckled.

"Well, sweetie, call if you find out something?"

"Okay."

We hung up and I had gone into the TV lounge to check and see if any loose papers might happen to have Andrew Vista's name on it. Nothing. I massaged my head 'cause I was beginning to get annoyed. Then I walked into the kitchen and simmered some hot water for a cup of tea to calm my nerves. I sat on the bar stool tapping my fingers on the table. My brain was fried. Then an idea hit me so I picked up the phone and called Manhattan at work.

"Brookedale's, Home Décor, Manhattan Mansfield speaking, how may I help you?"

"Manhattan, act like you're ill and come by. I need your help!"

Manhattan used her drama skills from high school and started gagging like she was about to vomit. I pressed my ear to the phone and overheard a woman asking if she was okay.

"Oh, I'm not feeling well. Oh, my stomach. I think I'm gonna go home." I heard Manhattan say. Then Manhattan whispered in the receiver, "I'm on my way."

We hung up and I paced the floor until she arrived.

Manhattan arrived and I buzzed her in. Minutes

later she knocked on the door. As I opened it she was huffing out of breath and rushed into my apartment and plopped her Burberry bag on the end table, and sat down on the sofa.

"Embellish, what's wrong?!"

I sat down and explained that I thought London was being deceitful. I told her about the lawyer he hired and how he went behind my back with his mother. I rubbed my eyes. "Who's the lawyer?" Manhattan asked.

"Some guy named, Andrew Vista. Have you heard of him?"

"No. Do you have a number for him?"

"Fernando found a business card of his at the gallery. Let me call and get it."

I picked up the phone and spoke briefly with Fernando.

"Here's the number." I paused. "Manhattan I need to know why he changed lawyers and never told me. It doesn't sound like something he would do. But his mother...."

I stopped in the middle of my sentence thinking of what momma had said. Find out what's going on first before jumping to conclusions. "Listen Manhattan, I wouldn't ask you to get involved but I need to find this Andrew Vista."

"Embellish, you know better than to think this is an imposition. Whatever you need I'm here to help. I think the first thing is meeting this Andrew Vista in person. I'm going to have to pretend that I need some legal advice. Hopefully he has free consultation. What's the number?"

I read the number off while Manhattan dialed. And I walked into the kitchen and picked up the phone to listen in.

"Andrew Vista's office, how may I help you?" A woman with a soft-spoken voice answered.

"Yes, I would like free consultation. Would I be able to speak with Mr. Vista, if I set an appointment?"

"Yes ma'am. He's here until 5:00 today, would you like me to fit you in around 3:00 o'clock?"

"Yes, please. My name is Autumn Chance. What is your address?"

"Do you have a pen and paper, ma'am?"

"Yes."

"The address is 500 Pigmonte Drive, Suite 3B, Paramus, New Jersey. You have to get on Route 17 North. Come all the way down until you see SYMS clothing store. The building is before SYMS, just park in the parking lot."

"Sure. Thank you."

We hung up.

"Girl, his office is in New Jersey…in Paramus off of Rt. 17 North. Why would he go to New Jersey?"

Manhattan had a puzzled look upon her face, too. I started pacing the living room floor, baffled.

"We have to be there at 3:00." Manhattan said.

"No, no, Manhattan, I can't go with you! You're gonna have to handle this on your own because I don't want him to see me. I need to dig a little deeper first. My gut tells me that there is more than meets the eye with this. Maybe I can have Fernando go with you. Let me call him."

I sat on the sofa and picked up the phone and called Fernando.

"ABstractions, Fernando speaking, how may I help you?"

"Fernando are you able to get away around two o'clock?"

"I'm afraid not, I have a potential buyer coming in today. Why, what's up?"

"Oh, I have Manhattan going to pay Mr. Vista a visit. His office is in New Jersey, and I wanted to know if you could go with her, but its okay."

"I'm sorry."

"Don't be."

We hung up and I remained seated thinking until Manhattan distracted my thoughts.

"Embellish, don't worry I'll be fine. Look at me, all this gorgeousness, please. As long as he is tall, dark, and handsome I'll have him eaten out of my hands."

We laughed.

"I need to know what type of service he gave London. Why was his mother there? Why would he switch lawyers? What's the big secret?!" I rubbed my eyes, again.

"I need to figure out an angle so that he doesn't get suspicious. This is not going to be easy trying to get him to spill the beans; you know that right, E?"

"Yeah. Everything is just so frustrating, you know? I can't call my mother-in-law to find out because she's not going to tell me."

"Sweetie, I'll do the best that I can, don't worry."

I cracked a smile.

"Now, you try and relax while I go home and get all gorgeous. I hope this man is not butt-ugly." Manhattan chuckled.

Manhattan left and I sat on the sofa pondering until I decided to tag along with her. I picked up the phone and reached her on her cell phone to let her know.

"Girl, I changed my mind. I'll meet you at your place in about an hour."

It was close to three o'clock when Manhattan and I arrived at Mr. Vista's suite. We sat in her car for a few minutes gathering our thoughts as she transformed herself into a delightful delicacy for Mr. Vista to marvel. She glided another coat of Nar lip-gloss on, unbuttoned two buttons on her silver Ann Taylor ruffle blouse showing a hint of cleavage. She unloosened her ponytail and shook her hair wildly. Then she changed from her low heel Nine West loafers into her Charles David stilettos accentuating her legs, making them look longer and sexier. She primped in the mirror a second more and then we exited her car.

As we walked into the office, we were greeted by a woman who sat behind a desk who we assumed was Mr. Vista's secretary. There was a nameplate on her desk that read, Kathryn Winters, middle-age woman with cashmere white skin, big beautiful blue eyes and curly dark black hair. Mrs. Winters asked us to have a seat and asked Manhattan to fill out a form about her reason for wanting consultation.

A few minutes after filling out the form the door opened to Mr. Vista's office, and a man stood in the doorway. Manhattan blinked twice hoping that her mouth was not dangling open. I was spellbound by his gorgeousness. Well, that was an understatement from what stood before me. A young Richard Gere was who he put me in mind of. The man looked savvy in his Italian cut Kenneth Cole gray slacks. *How many inches is he packing?*

Quickly my mind drifted back.

He was tall, medium build with muscles that detailed his pinstriped white and light gray dress shirt and rich leather black shoes.

"Ms. Chance." The man called out.

Manhattan stood up and so did I.

"Hi, I'm Mr. Vista."

Manhattan was speechless so I stepped in before she made a complete fool out of the both of us.

Snap out of it! My inner voice shouted at her.

"Hi, um, I'm Rachel Drumming and this is um, Autumn …."

I would love to give you a chance to rock my world, mister. My mind had a mind of its own. Naughty thoughts invaded me by his debonairness. Finally, Manhattan came to and put some oomph in her sway as we entered his office. I happened to turn my head as I caught Mrs. Winters turning, cutting her eyes, and smiling at Mr. Vista as if she said, "There's another one trying to fetch a man." And to my surprise, Mr. Vista nodded his head as if he agreed with her. Then we stepped into his office and he shut the door behind him.

"Please, have a seat, ladies."

Manhattan got all comfy and uppity. "Actually, it's Mrs."

"Oh, pardon me." Mr. Vista said.

"No problem." She puckered her glossy lips trying to entice him.

"So, Mrs. Chance, what can I help you with?"

Manhattan fell into a complete daze so I had to jump in, but before I could Mr. Vista had caught on that she was floating in outer space somewhere. I lowered my head so embarrassed.

"Mrs. Chance…Mrs. Chance, Are you okay?"

Manhattan came to and jumped back into character. "Oh, oh, yes." She cut her eyes and tilted her head to the side. "Um, what did you say?"

Mr. Vista sat on the edge of his desk and made eye contact with her.

I was floating in my own world. *God he's gorgeous. Do me? Do me right here and now! Knock all that shit off of your desk and strap me down and manhandle me like a beast in heat. Uh-oh, Pink Khocolate was stepping out and I had to tuck her ass back in before things got out of hand.*

"What can I assist you with?" Mr. Vista asked.

And again I fell into the trap with my filthy mind. *Some d.i.c.k… hurry! I'm horny!*

I nudged Manhattan with my elbow to bring her back to earth.

"Oh." Manhattan laughed trying to stick to the plan. Mr. Vista gazed into her eyes diligently waiting for a response.

"Well, um, Mr. Vista, my husband passed away and his partner inquired about what I was going to do about the business. I would rather keep it going since it's doing so well. It's a restaurant in New York, Squash, have you heard of it?"

"No, I can't say I have."

"Well, I discussed it with his partner that I would just transfer the names over, but I was wondering how I would go about it."

"Was your husband married before?"

"No, I was his only wife."

"Okay, well, it sounds like just a matter of drawing up some new forms and having both you and the existing partner sign on the dotted line stating that you are the new partners. I take it that your husband had everything pertaining to the restaurant in his name?"

"Yes, I wasn't really interested in it. I'm an interior designer. But after he died I got to thinking that I should keep it going. You know, as a remembrance of something he truly loved."

Mr. Vista drifted slightly and nodded his head.

"You can schedule an appointment with Mrs. Winters. I would be more than happy to assist you. If you can find any important papers in reference to the business agreement, please bring them with you along with your partner."

"Sure." Manhattan said, as she crossed her legs, flipped her hair, and leaned back trying to lure him in with her cleavage. I literally wanted to gag. My mind drifted again practically cussing Manhattan out.

Look, look, dammit! What is the problem? Cut the crap! This is business. Stick to the plan, I thought.

I leaned back in my seat and I observed Mr. Vista's

body language. He was not interested in Manhattan. Finally, I think she noticed as her eyes glanced over at a photo of him and a woman—a black woman who he was embraced in a hug with. Manhattan seemed a little disappointed after she viewed the photo. I smirked slightly as it was comical to me.

Manhattan stood and took another glance at the photo before we saw ourselves out.

"Thanks for your time, Mr. Vista. I'll be sure to make that appointment with Mrs. Winters." Manhattan pointed her index finger.

"You're welcome." He said, as he sat down at his desk.

Manhattan shut the door behind us and we bypassed Mrs. Winters, walked out of the building and into her car and drove off.

On our way back to New York I had an eerie feeling come over me as if London was speaking to my spirit and his voice was saying live in peace. *What did that mean*, I thought to myself. *Live in peace.* How was I supposed to do that with all of that confusion going on in my life? Whatever London was trying to say to me had an overwhelming impact on me so I turned and looked at Manhattan and said, "Prying won't do anything for me but possibly bring more pain into my life. Some things don't need to be known. I, for one know that to be true based on my past history."

Manhattan looked at me strangely, but she understood what I meant about my *past*. She never interrupted my train of thought. She just listened.

"I'm going to let Fernando handle his business with the gallery and if he needs me I'll be a phone call away. Manhattan, I need to move on in my life—starting today."

Manhattan nodded her head and laid her hand on top of mine as we headed to Napa Valley Grille for a bite to eat before heading back home.

When I arrived home I had this impulse to go into my bedroom, enter my closet and pull out my Pink BlackBerry. I charged her up. Why? I didn't know, but a lot was missing in my life and I thought I could somehow regain some sense of self. After about an hour it was fully charged. I pushed that one button to turn the power back on in me. Never did I think it would actually ring, but around 11:00 p.m. that night, it did. And I got back into character.

"Hel-lo. What's your pleasure?" The sensual cat was reborn.

"Ah, I'm looking for some companionship. Can we meet?" The man asked.

"Sure. But I would need your credit card number. Do you have Visa, American Express, MasterCard, or Discover?"

"American Express," he spoke in a mellow tone.

"What's the expiration date and the three digit security numbers on the back of your card?"

"11/20. And the three numbers are 111."

"Well, I can make reservations at the Summer Inn in Fort Lee."

"Sure. That would be fine." Again, he spoke softly.

"Well, I will put it under Pink Khocolate."

"Pink Khocolate," he repeated.

"Yes. Let's meet say around midnight."

"Midnight…is fine. Oh, Pink Khocolate what's your favorite flower?"

He caught me off guard with that question.

"My favorite flower?" I asked with a perplexing look on my face.

"Yes, your favorite flower: roses, lilies, dandelions, orchids, tulips?"

I never really took the time to think about what type of flowers I liked.

I shrugged my shoulders. "Ah, you surprise me."

"Sure. I'll surprise you."

And that he did.

Believe it or not that night I never left my apartment. And I never got off the phone with my potential client. Come to find out when he said that he wanted companionship that was exactly what he meant. He didn't want to have sex with me. He merely wanted to talk. Talk about love, loss, and life. He took me aback because it was the first time out of all the years that I had been a "Khocolate Companion" that someone actually cared about what was on my mind, and not my body. Even though I had aged I was flattered to have encountered such an unfamiliar feeling that made me feel valued. All those years of pain manifested into a night of utter pleasure. Yes, the kind of pleasure that stimulated my mind. My client and I had so much in common. We had both loved twice and lost twice. He was in his grieving stages and just needed a shoulder to lean on. How ironic that he chose to call me of all people.

After being on the phone for nearly two hours he had finally disclosed his name. To my surprise, it was Andrew Vista. I never told him that it was me on the other end of the phone. I just listened to him reminisce about his wife, the same woman in the picture. He shared how much he loved her in her most vulnerable stages of battling ovarian cancer. How he cherished the moments, hours, and minutes of each waking day to see her beautiful face. How he loved her with all of his heart and soul. How he missed her terribly.

The question that I had been dying to ask had finally escaped from my mouth.

"Andrew, may I ask you why did you call me to share your most intimate moments with?"

He paused for a brief moment and then responded.

"Two reasons. First, because I knew that you would make time for me. And second, because I felt you of all people would understand my grief. I would think that something traumatic occurred in your life for you to decide to do what you do—who better to talk to than you? You soothe your pains by pleasuring total strangers. You're exploiting your sacred body because you are hurting inside. You don't know how to handle what happened to you. That person tormented your sacred body leaving you bewildered about love, life, and death. Yes, I know how that dark side looks, smells, and tastes. I married her and she was a blessing in disguise underneath all of that heartache and pain laid a beautiful black flower in bloom. She was my black rose."

Tears slowly rolled down my face, mostly by the tone of his mellow voice that flowed through my entire body. For once I felt like someone finally understood what I had endured.

I sniffled.

"Why are you sad?" He asked. "It wasn't your fault. You were probably young and had no one you could trust. It changed who you were because you were lost within. I completely understand. You can now set yourself free. Know that it is not too late."

I bowed my head, as my right arm clenched my stomach so tightly because his words hit the core of me. It felt so good to hear those words.

After we hung up, I lay on the sofa and cried a much-needed cry. And then I had fallen asleep with a sense of peace in my heart.

***

Ring…Ring…Ring.

"Hello."

"Hello, yes may I speak with a Embellish Bleus, please?" A deep male voice spoke.

"Speaking." I said, somewhat baffled.

"Um, Mrs. Bleus, I am sorry to call you, but I must inform you of some disturbing news." He paused.

"Sir...Mister, um, what is this about?"

"Your mother. Ah, Ms. Bedell Godsend."

"Yessss." I felt a seasick feeling in my stomach. My legs felt like they wanted to buckle.

"Mrs. Bleus, I am a surgeon at Prophesize Hospital and Medical Center in Knock-Boots."

"Yes, what's wrong with my mother?" I swallowed and braced myself as I held onto the kitchen wall. I literally held my breath.

"I'm sorry to inform you that she was pronounced dead at 11:00 this morning. We were trying to reach next of kin all morning. We were fortunate enough to have a staff member here who knew your mother and gave us your name so the police and I tried to track you down. I didn't want them to come to your home unannounced. I felt it best that I call you personally."

There was silence.

I didn't know how to talk. It was like my voice box stopped working. Tears engulfed from my eyes as my vision blurred. All I remember doing was slowly falling to the floor like air had been let out of my body. My whole world had crumbled just that instantly.

"How? What happened?" I strained to get those words out.

"*They* were shot. Caught in the crossfire as they were walking down the street on Curbstone. It was a drive-by. I am so very sorry for your loss."

"*They*?" I blinked twice still flustered. "You said *they*."

"Yes, there was a young woman around the age of

169

thirty-three with her. She had Down syndrome. She died at the scene."

I closed my eyes so tightly wishing that I had gone blind. My chest tightened up on me, as I knew in my heart. I knew in my gut.

"Mrs. Bleus, um, I would need you to come to the hospital."

"I, I, I, I, um, of course, of course." I said, incoherently.

I took a moment after hanging up the phone. Deep down I felt like nothing mattered anymore. I mean whatever was going on with London didn't matter to me. What mattered was that I had experienced *love* for the first time in my life with someone who loved me for me. Not for what I had or for what I was willing to do to get what I needed. No. Nothing mattered anymore because at that moment of me hanging up the phone my life had changed twenty times over. I had to get a grip to go to Prophesize Hospital and Medical Center to identify my mother. Bedell bent over backwards to provide for me. She supported me through thick and thin. She worked two jobs to provide for the family. The woman who never asked for a dime because of that word called "pride" and always remained humble in times of distress. She was a blessing in disguise. So no, nothing mattered to me. Nothing.

I felt the urge to breakdown in my living room. In the kitchen. Bathroom. Bedroom. TV lounge. In the elevator. In the lobby. In the car. In the parking lot. Before I entered the hospital and while walking through the halls. Before approaching the nurse station to ask for directions as to where my momma's body was. A tall white man escorted me to the morgue. I had to brace myself before the doctor pulled back the white sheet that uncovered momma's stiff body. I felt that hardened rock lodged in my throat. I shut my eyes that overflowed with tears streaking my distraught face. But it didn't really, really hit me until I had asked the doctor if I could possibly see the victim who was shot and died at the scene—the young woman with Down syndrome.

He looked at me peculiarly at first. But there must've been a certain look in my eyes that possibly gave me away. That possibly read that I could have been that young woman's flesh and blood. I bowed my head in shame, but yet I still hadn't broken down.

The white doctor with the bluest eyes I had ever seen walked over to the next victim and he slowly pulled back the sheet as my eyes opened slowly, as I swallowed the spit that was clogging my airway, as I nearly gasped because she was the most beautiful product of life I could have ever birthed into this world. I knew without a shadow of a doubt that she was mine. We were practically identical twins. That was the moment that I broke down and had fallen to my knees asking God to forgive me for my sins. And in that moment the most profound thing had happened to me. Something I never saw coming. Something I always dreamt of.

As I was walking down the corridor there was a man waiting in front of the nurse's station, waiting for me. He identified himself as Hunter. How he knew who I was, was beyond me. He stopped me in the halls and I nearly passed out when he said that he was my father. There who stood before me was a *white* man with one blue eye and one green eye. He asked for a moment of my time, which I had given him. We strolled to the cafeteria and chatted over a cup of herbal tea and he enlightened me on my life as well as his.

It seemed Bedell and Hunter were soul mates, but his mother frowned upon him dating my mother because she was black, lived in the projects, and wasn't book educated as most. His mother made my mother's life a living hell and at the time Hunter was just enrolling in Pre-med school.

Hunter looked me dead in my eyes and spoke with such softness. "I asked your mother to give you both my last name. I asked your mother to go with me. I told her that I would take care of my family, but she declined. She said that she would be fine. That she wanted me to fulfill my dream of becoming a doctor. That she wouldn't stand in my way. She started dating some guy and she told Pretty-Boy that he was his father. She thought he was going to provide for the family, but apparently he didn't. I stayed in touch as much as I could. I even asked her to marry me, and she declined. She told me that I could do so much better than her. That she had nothing to offer me. That I was too bright for a woman like her. She said that my mother was right about her. Eventually I stopped waiting and moved on with my life. I'm happily married. I have three children. Well, one of my boys died."

"I'm sorry for your loss. I know how that feels. I lost my husband just recently." I said a bit uncomfortable.

Hunter hand rose and touched my hand and I could feel the warmth from his soul. He put me in mind of London. But then what really made me leap out of my skin and back in was when he reached into his wallet and showed me a picture of his deceased son. My heart nearly stopped beating. I thought after my mother's death, my daughter's death that I had suffered enormously, but I was so dead wrong. When I gazed at that picture I slumped over into a ball of hysteria as Hunter tried to hold me up.

There in plain view was a picture of my beloved husband, London Bleus.

"Oh, God, what have I done?" I muffled my screams.

There was this sick feeling that consumed my whole body. I rehearsed every moment of intimacy we had ever shared together. Every kiss. Every hug. Remembering the feel of his penis inside my walls—his lips upon my breasts—his tongue upon my clitoris. Instantly I wanted to vomit, but then Hunter saved me from myself. I had to calm down. It was most difficult. Hunter shared that out of the three children he had London was the only one who was not his biological son. Talk about a load lifted off of my chest. London was adopted.

Hunter smiled as he expressed so fatherly. "When I saw London in his ripped jeans, ketchup stained T-shirt, and holey sneakers standing in front of me hoping to be picked I knew that he was meant to be mine. We had something in common." Hunter nodded his head up and down.

"What was that?" I asked.

"One blue eye and one green."

We both smiled.

"Hunter was London adopted twice because his parents were at the funeral. I didn't see you there."

"They weren't his parents. They were his grandparents. And no, I wasn't there, but I had sent my wife, Penelope."

"Your wife." I said. "Would she happen to be tall, beautiful, almost the spitting image of Julia Roberts?"

"Kinda. Why do you *ask*?"

"Well, if it was her then she must've bought one of London's paintings, "A Mother's Womb."

He smiled. "Yes, she bought it as a gift for me. I have it hanging in our living room."

I sighed so deeply. Things were making more sense to me.

November 11th was a day to grieve and celebrate life. All those years I thought my father was a bum. I thought he was dead. And there he was a prominent surgeon at Prophesize Hospital and Medical Center in Knock-Boots, New York.

I laid momma and my daughter, Char to rest at Wyeth & Rice Cemetery. I wanted them close to me. I reflected back to the painting C. It began to make sense to me. *How did London know?* He never uttered a word. After everything I resumed a relationship with my father, Hunter B. I never heard or cared to hear from my brother, Pretty-Boy. That part of my life had died in the casket with Char and Bedell.

Here I was a bastard, a product of incest and a high-priced whore. And yet, God granted me many wishes probably late in life, but to me right on time because my time was surely running out of time, but I remained patient. At least I knew what it felt like to be loved. And I was forever grateful.

I left the hospital and as I was walking towards my car I could hear this soulful voice of Ledisi singing, "Lost & Found" coming from someone's car radio and I could so easily relate to her lyrics as if they were written for me. And I was hoping that someone would find me because I needed to be found. I needed a change. I was willing to make the first move and I knew that He wouldn't let me fall.

That Sunday I parked my car and walked into another church and I got baptized not certain of where this path would lead me, but I was willing to try to take myself to a higher level, instead of kneeling down to the same ole bullshit of stroking, sucking, and licking coochie for the rest of my life. I had accomplished much more than I bargained. But the ultimate of them all was that I found peace and happiness along my journey of finding love for self, others, and the most difficult was finding forgiveness. Without *faith* as my motherly nurturer I didn't think I would've made it this far. Without God as my protector I probably would still be hurting and living the life I left behind. And without me wanting to change I probably would be dead or so lost that I might as well have been dead. But I'm here: mind, body, and spirit. I'm here.

***

I give myself a pat on the shoulder to say, Everetta Dildo you are something else. Mrs. Lady, you did it! I smile so big and take a long deep breath because it surely was far from easy. It was a job in itself, but I feel proud of my accomplishments—so very proud.

I sit at my desk and click on *print* for the last few chapters to my manuscript, *Spittin' 'Em Out Like Babies.* I give myself two days to sit back and read it word for word before packaging it up and shipping it off to:

WM Publishing House
Time Square, Suite 666
New York, New York 10000
Attn: Hershel Jennings, Senior Editor

Flight Literary, LLC
1016 Hightower, Suite 111
New York, New York 10000
Attn: Julie Flight-Editor-Literary Agent

I enclose a personal letter to Julie and it reads:

Dear Julie,

I didn't think that I could do it, but you've always had faith in me. That's why I know Faith is a woman. She has to be because women are strong creatures. Julie, you pushed me to my limit, critiqued my writing, and voiced your opinion on ways for me to improve my storytelling. It was difficult being a novice at this authorship, but I realize why you pushed me so hard. There was more to me than meets the eye. And there was so much I needed and wanted to share with the world. My sole purpose is to help, heal those who live in pain. I have to come clean with you. The two-years I had to write this manuscript nothing was coming forth. I was suffering from writer's block. Julie, I only had two months to come up with a story. I grew desperate not wanting to let you down or myself. So I pushed myself to come up with a story. A message. And my creative juices did not fail me. It helped me to realize that I had a lot that was heavy on my heart and I needed to set some things free. I think I've accomplished my goal. And I thank you from the bottom of my heart.

It has been a pleasure knowing you and I hope to see this work in published form before it is too late. Hopefully it will inspire other women.

As of today, I am a changed woman because of it. And I can finally rest with a clear conscience and allow my body, mind, and soul a moment to catch up and recline in relaxation. It has been a long haul, but it was worth the wait.

Best,

Everetta Dildo

I grab my keys and tuck the package under my armpit as I head out the door and make my way to the post office.

When I arrive at the post office I greet the young, mocha-complexioned clerk and hand her the package as she weighs it. That package seems so heavy and ironically it really is. The contents in it are priceless to me. So priceless that I pull off my straw hat and expose my baldness. The clerk looks at me somewhat caught off guard, but doesn't gawk at me like I am some alien from outer space. She smirks and places my change in the bin as my fingers scoop it out. I wait for my confirmation slip and then walk out the door with my head held high.

When I return home and I go into the TV lounge and sit in London's chair. Yes, my actual beloved husband. Gosh, I miss him.

Before I get comfy I go into the bedroom and I remove the book, *Invisible Man,* from the edge of the bed and walk back towards the TV lounge, and before I enter the lounge, I grab his dashiki off the chair, then I return back to the TV lounge and sit down and open the book to page 161. I lean back and sniff his scent from his dashiki and close my eyes in reminiscence of those good ole days. Then my smile turns into a frown as my right hand rises to feel where my left breast used to reside, a tear rolls down my face. I feel so proud to have lived long enough to tell this story. I exhale.

I think about my best friend, Manhattan Mansfield. Yes, that was her real name and I whisper in a soft-spoken voice, "thank you, Manhattan. Thanks for being a true friend." Then I exhale, as my eyes don't deceive me. *London.* He stands before me. Oh, my goodness! Tears stream down my face in disbelief. All these years, why now? I blink to make sure I am not hallucinating. My hands reach out as my body shakes so full of skepticism. My fingers touch my lips. *Oh, his face is so full of life.* My fingers tremble. *Oh, he looks so good.* My eyelids flutter as my heart skips a beat. Indeed, confession is good for the soul.

***

One week later...

Ring...Ring...Ring.

"Hi, this is Everetta I am not able to take your call at the moment. Please leave at message at the beep? God Bless."

"Everetta, its Julie, I received the package. I was so engrossed in this story. I must admit it caught me by surprised, but I love the originality. Oh Everetta, I didn't know. I am so sorry, so very sorry. Yes, this is a much-needed story for young girls and women. It will be a published work-of-art I just know it! I am so proud of you. Call me as soon as you get in so we can schedule our first meeting to get this book in print. And I adore the title, *Spittin' 'Em Out Like Babies*, where did you come up with such a usual title? Oh, we have so much to discuss. Call me!"

***

JACOB JAVITS, NYC

One year later...

In honor of:

MAGNIFICIENT WOMEN of COLOR

Guest Speaker: Julie Flight

Julie stands her five foot four inches in a coral-pink skirt suit with oyster pearls dangling from around her thick neck and clip on earrings to match. Her fiery red hair is pushed back with a pearl beaded headband and tucked behind her small ears, curled under at the nape of her neck. She takes one deep breath, stares out into the audience with her bright blue eyes, and gently puckers her salmon pink lipstick lips as she adjusts her bifocals. "Good Evening." Inhale. Exhale. She lifts her head up high and says, "I am honored to be here at the Jacob Javits Convention to accept this award on behalf of my dear friend Everetta Dildo. It devastated me to hear that Everetta Dildo had died. She was a woman of great integrity. Everetta had a creative mind and soulful spirit. She was a very courageous woman who had been battling breast cancer for years. But Everetta never let that stop her from pursuing her dream of becoming a known author.

"I just want to share something with you all. Everetta had two years to complete this manuscript. But she suffered from writer's block and was too embarrassed to tell me. So she pushed herself for two months so that I wouldn't be disappointed and neither would she. She challenged herself and I guess the challenge led to this testament of life. Of how this woman in the story endured much pain and suffering during her childhood into her adulthood. It makes me realize during traumatic experiences one encounters sometimes it is most difficult to admit that you were this person.

"In Everetta's case this was so because she was a

white woman who had lived a horrific life. A woman, who had been ridiculed by her parents for dating an African-American man, she fell deeply in love with him and later married him. Everetta was a product of foster care as a child into teen and she was placed in multicultural families. She had endured a lot, but what kept her grounded was friendship. As you read you will come to discover what friendship really meant to her. Even though it is not stated Everetta left a message behind for her best friend Manhattan Mansfield. She chose to tell her best friend's story because she felt it would empower other African-American women who have lived Manhattan's life, as well as hers. Yes, she combined both of their lives as one.

"Everetta wanted Manhattan to know that she should not be embarrassed about how her life used to be because she is a changed woman because of it. People do change from their hardships. Their struggles become their strengths. Manhattan apparently had many, many struggles, but Everetta revealed the truth in order for her best friend to continue on with life. Everetta divulged her best friend's secrets in order to *help* cleanse Manhattan's soul and to inspire others.

"With that being said in Everetta Dildo's memory I present this award to Manhattan Mansfield, *Spittin' 'Em Out Like Babies,* to all women who have faced physical, sexual, emotional, and mental abuse in their lives."

The audience gives a standing ovation as Manhattan stands to her feet in awe. Tears overflow from her eyes as she proceeds to walk onstage in a beautiful Vera Wang black dress. Her dreadlocks are tied back in a polished bun and her makeup is flawless. She takes several deep breaths, dabs her eyes with her white hanky and speaks in a crackling voice.

"Um, I, I, just want to say with all sincerity, 'Thank

you, Everetta because I couldn't have done it without you. For those of you who don't know, um, Everetta was like a sister to me. We bonded as good friends at Broke-Down Housing Projects in Knock-Boots. I couldn't believe a white girl wanted to be my best friend. But she did. And she didn't care what people thought, either.

"Everetta took time to get to know me—a troubled black girl from the hood. She showered me with love. I always envied her because she had spunk. She knew what she wanted and how she was going to get it. Everetta was different. And I began to like different, again. She was the only person I could confide in about my life. I had to get it out because it was literally eating me up inside. She never judged me for my indiscretions. And I loved her dearly for that. Sometimes a person feels ashamed of the way their life had been. And sometimes they don't know exactly how to make things right. But Everetta figured out a way to make the wrongs right for me. She's given me a precious gift that I will treasure for always.'"

Manhattan sighs and dabs her eyes and nose with her hanky.

"Yes. I remember when Everetta and I pledged over Oreo cookies and a glass of milk to remain friends, no matter what. We both kept our promises. I'm glad that Everetta got tired for me. I'm glad she chose to help free *my* soul and wrapped *my* story in Embellish B.

"Yes." I lower my head. I lift it up feeling proud. "Everetta Dildo will truly be missed, but she leaves a strong…." I pause. My lips quiver.

In a crackling voice I say, "Let me not forget the man who brought forth pleasure and peace in my life. The man Everetta named Boulevard Thrillman ended up being the man I married. His real name was Hershel Jennings. I was truly blessed to have a good man enter my life. I never thought in a million years that Hershel would ask me to marry him, but he did. That changed me for the better. Years later we divorced and later lost touch of one another." I lower my head and smile. Then lift it back up with a look of gratitude on my face. "Yes, Everetta leaves a strong and profound message behind—a testament of *our* lives.

"Thank you."

I arrive home and I plop on the couch feeling awkward about my past life. I have no regrets of Everetta divulging my story. Not one bit. It was necessary. I smile.

I raise my body and go into the kitchen for my meds. Lord knows I have a lot on my plate. It is exhausting dealing with life, but what can I do. So much has happened in my life—so much bad. I am lucky to be alive. *God is so good*, I think to myself.

I walk into my bedroom and enter my walk-in closet and reach on the top shelf for my silver box with key and open it. It is filled with letters that Hershel used to write me when we first started seriously courting. Those letters used to make me weep so full of joy for that man. I miss him dearly.

As I am rummaging through the love letters I come across an essay I wrote. I unfold it and begin to read it aloud as I did in front of my sixth grade class.

I chuckle remembering the look on my teacher Mrs. Bernice's face when I said the word *pussy*. I didn't get in trouble because she said it was part of my expression. That was the first time I was able to get some of the pain out. If only I could've confided in her. I tried giving hints with the essay but Mrs. Bernice never caught on. She just figured it was my creative juices flowing. But it wasn't that. It was the pain speaking with words. That was the only way I felt I could tell her. I was hoping that she would pull me to the side and ask me what brought on this work-of-art, but instead she praised me a job well done. I was beside myself, so shaken up.

The phone rings.

"Hello."

There is silence.

"Hello," I say again.

"Hello Manhattan."

My eyes widen, "Hershel?"

"Yes."

I smirk. "This is certainly a surprise hearing from you."

"Well, um, yes, I'm sure it is. I just wanted to congratulate you on your upcoming book."

"How do you know about my book?"

"Small world."

"What do you mean small world?"

"Well, I heard your speech. It was quite moving. Um, I didn't know until then. I work for WM Publishing House, as a senior editor. I read the manuscript that Everetta Dildo wrote. She was aware that I worked for WM Publishing House. We met, um; we met through a mutual friend. Well, before she died she sent me an email wanting me to *specifically* read the manuscript. She never said why. I never asked. Business was business. Um, Manhattan, I'm sorry I was never there for you. I guess I didn't understand a lot of what you were and had gone through. I wished that we had better communication maybe...."

I smile. Then take a deep breath as tears flow down my face.

"Hershel, I've longed to hear those words from you.

Thank you."

"Ah, don't thank me as of yet. Um, I called to tell you personally that we've decided not to print *Spittin' 'Em Out Like Babies*. Conflict of interest, you might say."

My smile turns upside down.

"Whose *we*?"

There is silence.

"Whose idea was that Hershel?" I sway my head from side to side. Unbelievable, I say to myself. "It's okay. I get it. But you get this! I have a copy of the manuscript. And since I have a job and a little money saved up I'll do the book myself. You won't stop me. You won't hinder my progression because of your ego. Because you're embarrassed of me...of whom I used to be. What is this revenge because I never told you about my past?"

There is silence.

"So that's it!"

Hershel sighs and whispers out his words. "You think I want people to know that my wife—"

"Ex-wife!" I exclaim.

"Need I remind you—,"

"Remind me of what, Hershel?" I say, with a crumpled forehead.

"When we met you were a lost puppy from the ghetto. I molded you into a woman of substance."

"Oh really. Newsflash, as I recall, mister, you molded all the ladies you indulged in. See I knew when we met that you had a wandering eye. I knew that I was not the only cat you were sniffing because you were too coy. You were too cocky about yourself. All the times you would disappear and then reappear, as if everything was supposed to be fine. And as long as I allowed it, hon, you kept on doing you until I got fed up with the bullshit."

"Listen Manhattan, you are my ex-wife, do you think I want everyone to look at you in a different light. Think about what you are about to do."

"Oh, so you are concerned about me?! Please, Hershel, save that for those snooty people at your job because I am not convinced. This is not about me; it's about you, as always. Here I thought you actually had an ounce of sensitivity, but I guess that's something that won't change with you. It's always about what others may think. Well, how do you think they will feel knowing that my husband was living on the "down low" with my best friend's husband? And as a result, all of us contracted the virus. You woulda thought with all the sucking and fucking I was doing, back in the day that one of those men would've done this to me, but no, it was my *husband*. MY HUSBAND! What would they think to know that the black man on campus was getting fucked up the ass? The man I cherished with all of my heart and soul. What you think I'm going to be like La Joyce Brookshire who wrote *Faith Under Fire Betrayed by a Thing Called Love* or Brenda Stone Browder who wrote *On the Up and Up: A Survival Guide for Women Living with Men on the Down Low* about how my husband betrayed me! How he never told me that he liked *men*! That he slept with *men* and as a result I am HIV-positive! Yes, Hershel, what will the people think if they knew about your dark secret? About how you are profiling and walking around undetected with the virus. See, you're always trying to keep up this image. You are a fraud. A coward." I vigorously shake my head from side to side. 'You were just spittin' 'em out like babies too, weren't you? No, no. You won't dissolve my voice to help others. This is about me, not you. Everetta didn't disclose anything about your indiscretions—about how London and you bonded. No, she loved that man to death. And she would never tarnish what he gave her. But you, you are a selfish son-of-a-bitch! No, Hershel, you won't silence me. You won't! You still can't accept me for me, huh? Like...like I am poison. But you did this to me remember? After all these years—'"

I pause to catch my breath.

"Know this, Hershel. *Spittin' 'Em Out Like Babies* will get published before you can even say, 'I do.' Yes, I know that you are planning on getting married to that skank transsexual you left me for. Tell her I said she can have my leftovers 'cause you ain't doing nothing but rotting away." *CLICK!*

I feel like I want to break down to my knees and bawl, but I don't. It is time to toughen up because life is just beginning for me. Even though I am sick it is not "the end" of the world for me. I've found my sole purpose and I am going to use it up until it *sucks* the life outta me. I nod my head up and down realizing that I am blessed because even though I lived a different lifestyle, back in the day, God had spared me from disease. It wasn't until after I got *me* together that my life became a nightmare. I thought I had dodged that bullet, but I guess I let love in and now it is slowly trying to take me out. Regardless of what is known I am still proud of myself. I have longed forgiven Hershel and I accept this life that I have. Why? That is so easy to answer, because it is still a life—my life. I have ten fingers, ten toes, mobility, sight, hearing, stable health, and most importantly a voice. I am truly, truly blessed to be alive.

"There is such a bed of black roses
A life of heartache and wretchedness
I am a sounding voice for those
who've pricked their tiny fingers
with spike thorns
bleeding to be believed."

About the Author

Karla Denise Baker is the authoress of *Anonymous* and *Sleepin' Wit' the Virus*. She resides in Paterson, New Jersey, with her son. Currently she is working on her next book.

To email: karlabkr@yahoo.com